William H. Waddell

A Latin Grammar for Beginners

William H. Waddell

A Latin Grammar for Beginners

ISBN/EAN: 9783337311353

Printed in Europe, USA, Canada, Australia, Japan

Cover: Foto ©Andreas Hilbeck / pixelio.de

More available books at **www.hansebooks.com**

A LATIN GRAMMAR

FOR BEGINNERS.

By WILLIAM HENRY WADDELL,

PROFESSOR OF ANCIENT LANGUAGES IN THE UNIVERSITY OF GEORGIA;

AUTHOR OF

"A GREEK GRAMMAR FOR BEGINNERS."

NEW YORK:

HARPER & BROTHERS, PUBLISHERS,

FRANKLIN SQUARE.

1871.

PREFACE.

THIS book is a companion to a "Greek Grammar for Beginners" by the same author. In many instances precisely the same words have been used in both books. The design of both is identically the same, viz., to furnish a book which shall contain no notes, remarks, observations, "*fine print*," in short, to be marked by a teacher for omission, but only essential and elementary principles and paradigms, which are to be thoroughly memorized by the pupil, without any exception whatever. The Grammar is designed to be committed to memory, from cover to cover, the first time the pupil goes over it. While mainly intended for use in the school-room, it is believed that it will be found sufficiently full for the purposes of the lower classes in our American colleges.

University of Georgia, Athens, Ga., *February*, 1871.

CONTENTS.

A LATIN GRAMMAR FOR BEGINNERS.

PART I.—ORTHOGRAPHY.

THE LATIN ALPHABET.

1. The Latin Alphabet consists of twenty-five letters, which are written and pronounced as follows, viz.:

A a (long),	pronounced like	a	in Father,	as Amāre.
A a (short),	" "	a	in Sat,	as Adeo.
B b,	" "	b	in Beet,	as Beatus.
C c (hard),	" "	c	in Cat,	as Callidus.
C c (soft),	" "	c	in Cinder,	as Cinis.
D d,	" "	d	in Dome,	as Domus.
E e (long),	" "	ā	in Māde,	as Lēnis.
E e (short),	" "	e	in Set,	as Lĕgo.
F f,	" "	f	in Fame,	as Fama.
G g (hard),	" "	g	in Gift,	as Gracilis.
G g (soft),	" "	g	in Gem,	as Gero.
H h,	" "	h	in Home,	as Honor.
I i (long),	" "	i	in Machīne,	as Pīnus.
I i (short),	" "	i	in Pin,	as Piscĭs.
J j,	" "	j	in Join,	as Jus.
K k,	" "	k	in Kiss,	as Kalendæ.
L l,	" "	l	in Late,	as Longus.
M m,	" "	m	in Moon,	as Moneo.
N n,	" "	n	in Noon,	as Novus.
O o (long),	" "	o	in Bone,	as Ōro.
O o (short),	" "	o	in Not,	as Bŏnus.
P p,	" "	p	in Probe,	as Peto.
Q q,	" "	q	in Queen,	as Qui.
R r,	" "	r	in Rest,	as Reddo.
S s,	" "	s	in Set,	as Sanus.
T t,	" "	t	in Top,	as Tabella.
U u (long),	" "	u	in Rūle,	as Ūnus.
U u (short),	" "	u	in Shut,	as Ŭlŭla.
V v,	" "	v	in Vine,	as Valeo.
X x,	" "	x	in Box,	as Vox.
Y y,	" "	y	in Sylvan,	as Sylla.
Z z,	" "	z	in Zone,	as Zona.

2. These letters are divided into Vowels and Consonants.

A, E, I, O, U, and Y are Vowels. The rest are Consonants.

3. Of the Consonants,

>Four are Liquids, viz., L, M, N, and R.
>Two are Spirants, viz., H and S.
>Two are Double Consonants, viz., X and Z.
>The remainder are Mutes.

DIPHTHONGS.

4. A Diphthong is the union of two vowels in one sound. The Diphthongs are ae, oe (often written together, æ, œ), ai, au, ei, eu, oi.

5. The Diphthongs are pronounced as follows, viz.:

>ae and oe like a̧ in Māde, as Poena.
>
>| ai | " | i | " | Shine, | " | Aulai. |
>| au | " | ou | " | Our, | " | Aula. |
>| ei | " | i | " | Mine, | " | Hei. |
>| eu | " | u | " | Tune, | " | Europa. |
>| oi | " | oi | " | Joy, | " | Oi. |

PART II.—ETYMOLOGY.

6. The Latin Language has Eight Parts of Speech, viz.: Nouns, Adjectives, Pronouns, Verbs, which are declined; and Adverbs, Prepositions, Conjunctions, and Interjections, which are not declined.

7. There are Three Persons: First, Second, and Third.

8. There are Three Genders: Masculine, Feminine, and Neuter.

(a) Names of Males, and of Rivers, Winds, and Months, are Masculine.

(b) Names of Females, and of Countries, Towns, and Trees, are Feminine.

(c) Indeclinable Nouns are Neuter.

Gender is also determined by termination.

9. There are Two Numbers: the Singular, denoting one; the Plural, denoting more than one.

10. There are Six Cases: the Nominative, Genitive, Dative, Accusative, Vocative, and Ablative.

11. There are Five Declensions: First, Second, Third, Fourth, and Fifth.

These Declensions are distinguished from each other by the following terminations of the Genitive Singular, viz.:

First Declension in		ae.
Second	"	" ī.
Third	"	" ĭs.
Fourth	"	" ūs.
Fifth	"	" eī.

SOME GENERAL RULES OF DECLENSION.

12. (a) The Accusative Singular ends always in m, except in some Neuters.

(b) The Vocative Singular is like the Nominative in all Latin Nouns, except those in us of the Second Declension.

(*c*) The Nominative and Vocative Plural end always alike.

(*d*) The Genitive Plural ends always in um.

(*e*) The Dative and Ablative Plural end always alike: in the First and Second Declensions, in is; in the Third, Fourth, and Fifth, in bus.

(*f*) The Accusative Plural ends always in s, except in Neuters.

(*g*) Nouns of the Neuter Gender have the Accusative and Vocative like the Nominative in both Numbers; and these Cases in the Plural end always in a.

13. The following Table exhibits a comparative view of the Five Declensions:

TERMINATIONS.

Singular.

I.	II. M.	N.	III. M.	N.	IV. M.	N.	V.
N. ă,	us, er, um,		—	—	us,	ŭ,	es,
G. æ,	ī,		is,		ūs,		eï,
D. æ,	ō,			ī,	uī,	ŭ,	eï,
A. am,	um,		em,	—	um,	ŭ,	em,
V. ă,	ĕ, er, um,		—	—	us,	ŭ,	es,
A. ā.	ō.		ĕ, or ī.			ū.	ē.

Plural.

I.	II.		III.		IV.		V.
N. æ,	ī,	ă,	es,	ă, iă,	us,	uă,	es,
G. ārum,	ōrum,		um, *or* ium,		uum,		ērum,
D. is,	is,		ĭbus,		ĭbus, *or* ŭbus,		ēbus,
A. as,	os,	ă,	es,	ă, iă,	us,	uă,	es,
V. æ,	ī,	ă,	es,	ă, iă,	us,	uă,	es,
A. is.	is.		ĭbus.		ĭbus, *or* ŭbus.		ēbus.

14. The Stem of a Noun is found by striking off the termination of the Genitive Singular. The above terminations added to the remainder will give the Cases of any Noun.

FIRST DECLENSION.

15. Nouns of the First Declension end in
ă and ē, which are Feminine, and in
ās and ēs, which are Masculine.

Regular Latin Nouns end only in a, and are declined
as follows:

Stella, *a star*, Feminine.

Singular.		Plural.	
N. stell ă,	*a star.*	N. stell ae,	*stars.*
G. stell ae,	*of a star.*	G. stell ărŭm,	*of stars.*
D. stell ae,	*to a star.*	D. stell īs,	*to stars.*
A. stell ăm,	*a star.*	A. stell ās,	*stars.*
V. stell ă,	*thou star!*	V. stell ae,	*ye stars!*
A. stell ă,	*with a star.*	A. stell īs,	*with stars.*

In like manner decline—

Acerra, *a censer.* Athlēta, m., *a wrestler.* Căsa, *a cottage.*
Acta, *the shore.* Aula, *a hall.* Castănea, *a chestnut.*
Æra, *a period of time.* Aura, *a breeze.* Cătăpulta, *an engine to*
Ærumna, *toil.* Aurīga, m., *a charioteer.* *cast darts.*
Agricŏla, *a husbandman.* Avia, *a grandmother.* Cătēna, *a chain.*

16. Greek Nouns in ūs, ēs, a, and ē are thus declined:

Sing.	Sing.	Sing.	Sing.
N. Ænĕās,	N. Anchīsĕs,	N. Medĕa,	N. Penelŏpē,
G. Ænĕæ,	G. Anchīsæ,	G. Medĕæ,	G. Penelŏpēs,
D. Ænĕæ,	D. Anchīsæ,	D. Medĕæ,	D. Penelŏpē,
A. Ænĕām,	Å. Anchīsēn,	A. Medĕan,	A. Penelŏpēn,
or Ænĕān,	V. Anchīsē,	*or* Medĕam,	*or* Penelŏpēm,
V. Ænĕā,	A. Anchīse.	V. Medĕa,	V. Penelŏpē,
A. Ænĕā.		A. Medĕa.	A. Penelŏpē.

SECOND DECLENSION.

17. Nouns of the Second Declension end in
ĕr, ĭr, ŭs, ŏs, which are Masculine, and in
ŭm and ŏn, which are Neuter.

Regular Latin Nouns end only in ĕr, ĭr, ŭs, ŭm, and are
declined as follows:

18.   *Singular.*

Man.	*Book.*	*Slave.*	*War.*
N. vĭr,	lĭbĕr,	servŭs (ŏs),	belĭŭm,
G. vĭr ĭ,	libr ĭ,	serv ĭ,	bell ĭ,
D. vĭr ŏ,	libr ŏ,	serv ŏ,	bell ŏ,
A. vĭr ŭm,	libr ŭm,	serv ŭm,	bell ŭm,
V. vĭr,	liber,	serv ĕ,	bell ŭm,
A. vĭr ŏ.	libr ŏ.	serv ŏ.	bell ŏ.

Plural.

N. vĭr ĭ,	libr ĭ,	serv ĭ,	bell ă,
G. vĭr ōrŭm,	libr ōrŭm,	serv ōrŭm,	bell ōrŭm,
D. vĭr ĭs,	libr ĭs,	serv ĭs,	bell ĭs,
A. vĭr ōs,	libr ōs,	serv ōs,	bell ă,
V. vĭr ĭ,	libr ĭ,	serv ĭ,	bell ă,
A. vĭr ĭs.	libr ĭs.	serv ĭs.	bell ĭs.

In like manner decline—

Arbĭtĕr, *a judge.*	Folĭum, *a leaf.*	Socer, *a father-in-law.*
Bĕllum, *war.*	Gladĭus, *a sword.*	Tĕlum, *a dart.*
Cădus, *a cask.*	Lūpus, *a wolf.*	Torus, *a couch.*
Cĕrvus, *a stag.*	Mūrus, *a wall.*	Tectum, *the roof.*

19. Greek nouns in os and on are thus declined:

Sing.	Sing.	Sing.	Plur.
N. Andrŏgĕōs,	N. Dēlŏs,	N. Mausōlĕon,	N. Mausōlĕa,
G. Andrŏgĕī,	G. Deli,	G. Mausōlĕo,	G. Mausōlĕon,
— Andrŏgĕō,	D. Delō,	D. Mausōlĕo,	D. Mausōlēis,
D. Andrŏgĕō,	A. Delŏn,	A. Mausōlĕon,	A. Mausōlĕa,
A. Andrŏgĕōn,	V. Delĕ,	V. Mausōlĕon,	V. Mausōlĕa,
— Andrŏgĕō,	A. Delō.	A. Mausōlĕo.	A. Mausōlēis.
V. Andrŏgĕōs,			
A. Andrŏgĕō.			

THIRD DECLENSION.

20. Nouns of the Third Declension ending in

o, er, or, es (increasing in the Genitive), and os, are Masculine,

as, es (*not* increasing in the Genitive), is, ys, s (preceded by a consonant), and x, are Feminine,

c, a, l, e, t, ar, men, ur, us, i, and y, are Neuter.

The pupil may fasten these terminations in his memory
by noting the sounds of the letters pronounced together;
for instance, in the Masculine endings, o, error, es, and
os; in the Neuter, cal-et-ar-men-ur-us, i, and y.

21. Nouns of this Declension are declined as follows:

	Sing.		Plur.	
N.	urb-s (f.),	a city.	urb-ēs,	cities.
G.	urb-ĭs,	of a city.	urb-ium,	of cities.
D.	urb-ĭ,	to or for a city.	urb-ĭbŭs,	to or for cities.
A.	urb-em,	a city.	urb-ēs,	cities.
V.	urb-s,	O city. [city.	urb-ēs,	O cities.
A.	urb-ē,	by, with, or from a	urb-ĭbŭs,	by, with, or from cities.
N.	princep-s (c.),	a chief.	princĭp-ēs,	chiefs.
G.	princĭp-ĭs,	of a chief.	princĭp-um,	of chiefs.
D.	princĭp-ĭ,	to or for a chief.	princĭp-ĭbŭs,	to or for chiefs.
A.	princĭp-em,	a chief.	princĭp-ēs,	chiefs.
V.	princep-s,	O chief. [a chief.	princĭp-ēs,	O chiefs. [chiefs.
A.	princĭp-ē,	by, with, or from	princĭp-ĭbŭs,	by, with, or from
N.	aetā-s (f.),	an age.	aetāt-ēs,	ages.
G.	aetāt-ĭs,	of an age.	aetāt-um,	of ages.
D.	aetāt-ĭ,	to or for an age.	aetāt-ĭbŭs,	to or for ages.
A.	aetāt-em,	an age.	aetāt-ēs,	ages.
V.	aetā-s,	O age. [an age.	aetāt-ēs,	O ages.
A.	aetāt-ē,	by, with, or from	aetāt-ĭbŭs,	by, with, or from ages.
N.	lăp-ĭs (m.),	a stone.	lăpĭd-ēs,	stones.
G.	lăpĭd-ĭs,	of a stone.	lăpĭd-um,	of stones.
D.	lăpĭd-ĭ,	to or for a stone.	lăpĭd-ĭbŭs,	to or for stones
A.	lăpĭd-em,	a stone.	lăpĭd-ēs,	stones.
V.	lăpĭ-s,	O stone. [stone.	lăpĭd-ēs,	O stones.
A.	lăpĭd-ē,	by, with, or from a	lăpĭd-ĭbŭs,	by, with, or from stones.
N.	consŭl (m.),	a consul.	consŭl-ēs,	consuls.
G.	consŭl-ĭs,	of a consul.	consŭl-um,	of consuls.
D.	consŭl-ĭ,	to or for a consul.	consŭl-ĭbŭs,	to or for consuls.
A.	consŭl-em,	a consul.	consŭl-ēs,	consuls.
V.	consŭl,	O consul. [consul.	consŭl-ēs,	O consuls. [suls.
A.	consŭl-ē,	by, with, or from a	consŭl-ĭbŭs,	by, with, or from con-
N.	clămŏr (m.),	a shout.	clămŏr-ēs,	shouts.
G.	clămŏr-ĭs,	of a shout.	clămŏr-um,	of shouts.
D.	clămŏr-ĭ,	to or for a shout.	clămŏr-ĭbŭs,	to or for shouts.
A.	clămŏr-em,	a shout.	clămŏr-ēs,	shouts.
V.	clămŏr,	O shout. [shout.	clămŏr-ēs,	O shouts. [shouts.
A.	clămŏr-ē,	by, with, or from a	clămŏr-ĭbŭs,	by, with, or from

	Sing.		Plur.	
N.	ansĕr (m.),	a goose.	ansĕr-ēs,	geese.
G.	ansĕr-ĭs,	of a goose.	ansĕr-um,	of geese.
D.	ansĕr-ī,	to or for a goose.	ansĕr-ĭbŭs,	to or for geese.
A.	ansĕr-em,	a goose.	ansĕr-ēs,	geese.
V.	ansĕr,	O goose. [goose.	ansĕr-ēs,	O geese.
A.	ansĕr-ĕ,	by, with, or from a	ansĕr-ĭbŭs,	by, with, or from geese.

N.	pătĕr,	a father.	patr-ēs,	fathers.
G.	patr-ĭs,	of a father.	patr-um,	of fathers.
D.	patr-ī,	to or for a father.	patr-ĭbŭs,	to or for fathers.
A.	patr-em,	a father.	patr-ēs,	fathers.
V.	pătĕr,	O father. [father.	patr-ēs,	O fathers.
A.	patr-ĕ,	by, with, or from a	patr-ĭbŭs,	by, with, or from fathers.

N.	crūs (n.),	a leg.	crūr-ă,	legs.
G.	crūr-ĭs,	of a leg.	crūr-um,	of legs.
D.	crūrī,	to or for a leg.	crūr-ĭbŭs,	to or for legs.
A.	crūs,	a leg.	crūr-ă,	legs.
V.	crūs,	O leg.	crūr-ă,	O legs.
A.	crūr-ĕ,	by, with, or from a leg.	crūr-ĭbŭs,	by, with, or from legs.

N.	ŏpŭs (n.),	a work.	ŏpĕr-ă,	works.
G.	ŏpĕr-ĭs,	of a work.	ŏpĕr-um,	of works.
D.	ŏpĕr-ī,	to or for a work.	ŏpĕr-ĭbŭs,	to or for works.
A.	ŏpŭs,	a work.	ŏpĕr-ă,	works.
V.	ŏpŭs,	O work. [work.	ŏpĕr-ă,	O works.
A.	ŏpĕr-ĕ,	by, with, or from a	ŏpĕr-ĭbŭs,	by, with, or from works.

N.	corpŭs (n.),	a body.	corpŏr-ă,	bodies.
G.	corpŏr-ĭs,	of a body.	corpŏr-um,	of bodies.
D.	corpŏr-ī,	to or for a body.	corpŏr-ĭbŭs,	to or for bodies.
A.	corpŭs,	a body.	corpŏr-ă,	bodies.
V.	corpŭs,	O body. [body.	corpŏr-ă,	O bodies. [bodies.
A.	corpŏr-ĕ,	by, with, or from a	corpŏr-ĭbŭs,	by, with, or from

N.	căpŭt (n.),	a head.	căpĭt-ă,	heads.
G.	căpĭt-ĭs,	of a head.	căpĭt-um,	of heads.
D.	căpĭt-ī,	to or for a head.	căpĭt-ĭbŭs,	to or for heads.
A.	căpŭt,	a head.	căpĭt-ă,	heads.
V.	căpŭt,	O head. [head.	căpĭt-ă,	O heads.
A.	căpĭt-ĕ,	by, with, or from a	căpĭt-ĭbŭs,	by, with, or from heads. .

Bōs, *an ox or cow.*

	Sing.	Plur.		Sing.	Plur.
N.	bōs,	bŏvēs.	A.	bŏvem,	bŏvēs.
G.	bŏvĭs,	bŏvum, or bŏum.	V.	bōs,	bŏvēs.
D.	bŏvī,	bōbŭs, or būbŭs.	A.	bŏvĕ,	bōbŭs, or būbŭs.

Vīs (*f.*), *strength.*

Sing.	Plur.	Sing.	Plur.
N. vīs,	vīrēs.	A. vim,	vīrēs.
G. (wanting)	vīrĭum.	V. (wanting)	vīrēs.
D. (wanting)	vīrĭbŭs.	A. vī,	vīrĭbŭs.

	Sing.		Plur.
N. dux (*c.*),	*a leader.*	dŭc-ēs,	*leaders.*
G. dŭc-ĭs,	*of a leader.*	dŭc-um,	*of leaders.*
D. dŭc-ī,	*to or for a leader.*	dŭc-ĭbŭs,	*to or for leaders.*
A. dŭc-em,	*a leader.*	dŭc-ēs,	*leaders.*
V. dux,	*O leader.* [*leader.*	dŭc-ēs,	*O leaders.*
A. dŭc-ē,	*by, with,* or *from a*	dŭc-ĭbŭs,	*by, with,* or *from leaders.*

N. lex (*f.*),	*a law.*	lēg-ēs,	*laws.*
G. lēg-ĭs,	*of a law.*	lēg-um,	*of laws.*
D. lēg-ī,	*to or for a law.*	lēg-ĭbŭs,	*to or for laws.*
A. lēg-em,	*a law.*	lēg-ēs,	*laws.*
V. lex,	*O law.*	lēg-ēs,	*O laws.*
A. lēg-ē,	*by, with,* or *from a law.*	lēg-ĭbŭs,	*by, with,* or *from laws.*

N. mīlĕ-s (*m.*),	*a soldier.*	mīlĭt-ēs,	*soldiers.*
G. mīlĭt-ĭs,	*of a soldier.*	mīlĭt-um,	*of soldiers.*
D. mīlĭt-ī,	*to or for a soldier.*	mīlĭt-ĭbŭs,	*to or for soldiers.*
A. mīlĭt-em,	*a soldier.*	mīlĭt-ēs,	*soldiers.*
V. mīlĕ-s,	*O soldier.* [*soldier.*	mīlĭt-ēs,	*O soldiers.* [*diers.*
A. mīlĭt-ē,	*by, with,* or *from a*	mīlĭt-ĭbŭs,	*by, with,* or *from sol-*

N. hiem-s (*f.*),	*winter.*	hiĕm-ēs,	*winters.*
G. hiĕm-ĭs,	*of winter.*	hiĕm-um,	*of winters.*
D. hiĕm-ī,	*to or for winter.*	hiĕm-ĭbŭs,	*to or for winters.*
A. hiĕm-em,	*winter.*	hiĕm-ēs,	*winters.*
V. hiom-s,	*O winter.* [*winter.*	hiĕm-ēs,	*O winters.* [*ters.*
A. hiĕm-ē,	*by, with,* or *from*	hiĕm-ĭbŭs,	*by, with,* or *from win-*

N. leo (*m.*),	*a lion.*	leōn-ēs,	*lions.*
G. leōn-ĭs,	*of a lion.*	leōn-um,	*of lions.*
D. leōn-ī,	*to or for a lion.*	leōn-ĭbŭs,	*to or for lions.*
A. leōn-em,	*a lion.*	leōn-ēs,	*lions.*
V. leo,	*O lion.*	leōn-ēs,	*O lions.*
A. leōn-ē,	*by, with,* or *from a lion.*	leōn-ĭbŭs,	*by, with,* or *from liors.*

N. virgo,	*a maiden.*	virgĭn-ēs,	*maidens.*
G. virgĭn-ĭs,	*of a maiden.*	virgĭn-um,	*of maidens.*
D. virgĭn-ī,	*to or for a maiden.*	virgĭn-ĭbŭs,	*to or for maide*
A. virgĭn-em,	*a maiden.*	virgĭn-ēs,	*maidens.*
V. virgo,	*O maiden.* [*maiden.*	virgĭn-ēs,	*O maidens.* [*ens.*
A. virgĭn-ē,	*by, with,* or *from a*	virgĭn-ĭbŭs,	*by, with,* or *from maid-*

	Sing.		Plur.	
N.	host-ĭs (c.),	an enemy.	host-ēs,	enemies.
G.	host-ĭs,	of an enemy.	host-ĭum,	of enemies.
D.	host-ī,	to or for an enemy.	host-ĭbŭs,	to or for enemies.
A.	host-em,	an enemy.	host-ēs,	enemies.
V.	host-ĭs,	O enemy. [enemy.	host-ēs,	O enemies. [mies.
A.	host-ĕ,	by, with, or from an	host-ĭbŭs,	by, with, or from ene-
N.	nūb-ēs (f.),	a cloud.	nūb-ēs,	clouds.
G.	nūb-ĭs,	of a cloud.	nūb-ĭum,	of clouds.
D.	nūb-ī,	to or for a cloud.	nūb-ĭbŭs,	to or for clouds.
A.	nūb-em,	a cloud.	nūb-ēs,	clouds.
V.	nūb-ēs,	O cloud. [cloud.	nūb-ēs,	O clouds.
A.	nūb-ĕ,	by, with, or from a	nūb-ĭbŭs,	by, with, or from clouds.
N.	măr-ĕ (n.),	the sea.	măr-ĭă,	seas.
G.	măr-ĭs,	of the sea.	măr-ĭum,	of seas.
D.	măr-ī,	to or for the sea.	măr-ĭbŭs,	to or for seas.
A.	măr-ĕ,	the sea.	măr-ĭă,	seas.
V.	măr-ĕ,	O sea. [sea.	măr-ĭă,	O seas.
A.	măr-ī,	by, with, or from the	măr-ĭbŭs,	by, with, or from seas.
N.	ănĭmăl (n.),	an animal.	ănĭmāl-ĭă,	animals.
G.	ănĭmāl-ĭs,	of an animal.	ănĭmāl-ĭum,	of animals.
D.	ănĭmāl-ī,	to or for an animal.	ănĭmāl-ĭbŭs,	to or for animals.
A.	ănĭmăl,	an animal.	ănĭmāl-ĭă,	animals.
V.	ănĭmăl,	O animal. [animal.	ănĭmāl-ĭă,	O animals. [mals.
A.	ănĭmāl-ī,	by, with, or from an	ănĭmāl-ĭbus,	by, with, or from ani-
N.	nōmĕn (n.),	a name.	nōmĭn-ă,	names.
G.	nōmĭn-ĭs,	of a name.	nōmĭn-um,	of names.
D.	nōmĭn-ī,	to or for a name.	nōmĭn-ĭbŭs,	to or for names.
A.	nōmĕn,	a name.	nōmĭn-ă,	names.
V.	nōmĕn,	O name. [name.	nōmĭn-ă,	O names. [names.
A.	nōmĭn-ĕ,	by, with, or from a	nōmĭn-ĭbŭs,	by, with, or from
N.	fulgŭr (n.),	lightning.	fulgŭr-ă,	lightnings.
G.	fulgŭr-ĭs,	of lightning.	fulgŭr-um,	of lightnings.
D.	fulgŭr-ī,	to or for lightning.	fulgŭr-ĭbŭs,	to or for lightnings.
A.	fulgŭr,	lightning.	fulgŭr-ă,	lightnings.
V.	fulgŭr,	O lightning. [ning.	fulgŭr-ă,	O lightnings. [nings.
A.	fulgŭr-ĕ,	by, with, or from light-	fulgŭr-ĭbŭs,	by, with, or from light-
N.	calcăr (n.),	a spur.	calcăr-ĭă,	spurs.
G.	calcăr-ĭs,	of a spur.	calcăr-ĭum,	of spurs.
D.	calcăr-ī,	to or for a spur.	calcăr-ĭbŭs,	to or for spurs.
A.	calcăr,	a spur.	calcăr-ĭă,	spurs.
V.	calcăr,	O spur. [spur.	calcăr-ĭă,	O spurs.
A.	calcăr-ī,	by, with, or from a	calcăr-ĭbŭs,	by, with, or from spurs.

Sĕnex, *an old man.*

Sing.	Plur.
sĕnex,	sĕnēs.
sĕnĭs,	sĕnum.
sĕnī,	sĕnĭbŭs.
sĕnem,	sĕnēs.
sĕnex	sĕnēs.
sĕnĕ,	sĕnĭbŭs.

Jūpĭtĕr (=Jŏv-pĭtĕr, *i.e.* pătĕr),
(the god) Jupiter.

Jūpĭtĕr.
Jŏvĭs.
Jŏvī.
Jŏvem.
Jūpĭtĕr.
Jŏvĕ.

GREEK NOUNS OF THE THIRD DECLENSION.

22. The following Nouns exemplify all the forms of the declension of Greek Nouns of the Third Declension.

These Nouns have their Genitive in dis and dos:

Sing.	Sing.	Sing.	Plur.
N. Daphnĭs,	N. Bēlĭs,	N. Troăs,	N. Troădĕs,
G. Daphnĭdĭs,	G. Belĭdĭs,	G. Troădĭs,	G. Troădŭm,
Daphnĭdŏs,	Belĭdŏs,	Troădŏs,	Troădōn,
D. Daphnĭdĭ,	D. Belĭdĭ,	D. Troădĭ,	D. Troădĭbŭs,
A. Daphnĭm,	A. Belĭdĕm,	A. Troădĕm,	A. Troădăs,
Daphnĭn,	Belĭdă,	Troădă,	V. Troădĕs,
V. Daphnĭ,	V. Belĭ,	V. Troăs,	A. Troădĭbŭs.
Daphnĭdĕ.	A. Belĭdĕ.	A. Troădĕ.	

The following have their Genitive in ĭs, ŏs, or in ĭos and ўos; except Dido, which has the Genitive in us:

Sing.	Sing.	Sing.	Plur.
N. Orpheus,	N. Tĭphўs,	N. hærĕsĭs,	N. hærĕsēs-ĭs,
G. Orphĕ-os, ōs,	G. Tĭphўŏs,	G. hærĕsĭs,	G. hærĕsĭŭm,
D. Orphĕi-ĕŏ,	D. Tĭphўĭ,	hærĕsĭŭs,	hærĕsĭōn,
A. Orphĕ-a,	A. Tĭphўm,	hærĕsĕŭs,	hærĕsĕŏn,
V. Orpheu,	Tĭphўn,	D. hærĕsĭ,	D. hærĕsĭbŭs,.
A. Orphĕŏ.	V. Tĭphў,	A. hærĕsim,	
	A. Tĭph-ўĕ.	hærĕsin,	A. hærĕsĕas-ĭs,
		V. hærĕsĭ,	V. hærĕses-ĭs,
		A. hærĕsi.	A. hærĕsibŭs.

Sing.	Plur.	Sing.	Sing.
N. Arabs,	N. Arăbĕs,	N. Aër,	N. Dīdŏ,
G. Arăbĭs,	G. Arăbŭm, et	G. Aĕrĭs,	G. Dīdūs,
D. Arăbi,	Arăbōn,	D. Aeri,	D. Dīdŏ,
A. Arăbĕm, et	D. Arăbĭbŭs,	A. Aeră,	A. Dīdŏ,
Arăbă,	A. Arăbăs,	V. Aër,	V. Dīdŏ,
V. Arabs,	V. Arăbĕs,	A. Aĕrĕ.	A. Dīdŏ.
A. Arăbĕ.	A. Arăbĭbŭs.		

FOURTH DECLENSION.

23. Nouns of the Fourth Declension ending in
us are Masculine,
u are Neuter,
and are declined as follows:

	Sing.		Plur.	
N. grăd-ŭs (m.),	a step.	grăd-ūs,	steps.	
G. grăd-ūs,	of a step.	grăd-ŭum,	of steps.	
D. grăd-ŭī,	to or for a step.	grăd-ĭbŭs,	to or for steps.	
A. grăd-um,	a step.	grăd-ūs,	steps.	
V. grăd-ŭs,	O step. [a step.	grăd-ūs,	O steps.	
A. grăd-ū,	by, with, or from	grăd-ĭbŭs,	by, with, or from steps	

N. gĕn-ū,	a knee.	gĕn-ŭă,	knees.
G. gĕn-ūs,	of a knee:	gĕn-ŭum,	of knees.
D. gĕn-ū,	to or for a knee.	gĕn-ĭbŭs,	to or for knees.
A. gĕn-ū,	a knee.	gĕn-ŭă,	knees.
V. gĕn-u,	O knee.	gĕn-ŭă,	O knees.
A. gĕn-ū,	by, with, or from a knee.	gĕn-ĭbŭs,	by, with, or from knees.

In like manner decline:

acŭs, ūs, f.	a needle.	fructus, us, m.	fruit.
arcŭs, ūs, m.	a bow.	măgistrātus, us, m.	a magistrate.
auditus, ūs, m.	hearing.	mănus, us, f.	a hand.
cursus, ūs, m.	running.	pĕdĭtātus, us, m.	infantry.
ĕquĭtātus, ūs, m.	cavalry.	portus, us, m.	a harbor.
exercĭtus, us, m.	an army.	quercus, us, f.	an oak.
fĭcus, us, f.	a fig, fig-tree.	sensus, us, m.	a sense.

Dŏmŭs, f. a house (Second and Fourth Declensions).

Sing.	Plur.	Sing.	Plur.
N. Dŏmŭs,	Dŏmŭs.	A. Dŏmum,	Dŏmōs (rarely cŏmūr).
G. Dŏmŭs,	Dŏmŭum, or dŏmōrum.	V. Dŏmŭs,	Dŏmŭs.
D. Dŏmŭī,	Dŏmĭbŭs.	A. Dŏmō,	Dŏmĭbŭs.

FIFTH DECLENSION.

24. Nouns of the Fifth Declension end in es, and are of
the Feminine Gender.
They are thus declined:

Sing.		Plur.	
N. dĭ-ēs,	a day.	dĭ-ēs,	days.
G. dĭ-ēī,	of a day.	dĭ-ērum,	of days.
D. dĭ-ēī,	to or for a day.	dĭ-ēbŭs,	to or for days.
A. dĭ-em,	a day.	dĭ-ēs,	days.
V. dĭ-ēs,	O day.	dĭ-ēs,	O days.
A. dĭ-ē,	by, with, or from a day.	dĭ-ēbŭs,	by, with, or from days.

DECLENSION OF COMPOUND NOUNS.

25. When a Compound Noun consists of two Simple Nouns, both in the Nominative Case, both parts are declined; if only one part is in the Nominative, that alone is varied.

Rēs-pūblĭcă, a republic.	Jūs-jūrāndŭm, an oath.	Păter-fămĭlias, a father of a family.
Fem.	Neut.	Masc.
First and Fifth Dec.	Second and Third Dec.	First and Third Dec.

Sing.

N. rēs-pūblĭcă,	N. jūs-jūrāndŭm,	N. păter-fămĭlias,
G. rēi-pūblĭcæ,	G. jūrĭs-jūrāndī,	G. pătris-fămĭlias,
D. rēi-pūblĭcæ,	D. jūrĭ-jūrāndō,	D. pătri-fămillas,
A. rēm-pūblĭcam,	A. jūs-jūrāndŭm,	A. pătrem-fămĭlias,
V. rēs-pūblĭca,	V. jūs-jūrāndŭm,	V. păter-fămillas,
A. rē-pūblĭcā.	A. jūrĕ-jūrāndō.	A. pătre-fămĭlias.

Plur.

N. rēs-pūblĭcæ,	N. jūră-jūrāndă,	N. pătrēs-fămĭliārum,
G. rērum-pūblĭcārum,	G. jūrŭm-jūrāndŏrŭm,	G. pătrŭm-fămĭliārum,
D. rēbus-pūblĭcīs,	D. jūrĭbŭs-jūrāndīs,	D. pătrĭbus-fămĭliārum,
A. rēs-pūblĭcās,	A. jūră-jūrānda,	A. pătrēs-fămĭliārum,
V. rēs-pūblĭcæ,	V. jūră-jūrāndă,	V. pătrēs-fămĭliārum,
A. rēbus-pūblĭcīs.	A. jūrĭbŭs-jūrāndīs.	A. pătrĭbŭs-fămĭliārum.

ADJECTIVES.

26. Adjectives in Latin have three terminations, two terminations, and one termination. The first termination is Masculine, the second Feminine, and the third Neuter. They are of the First and Second Declensions, and of the Third Declension. They are declined as follows:

I. Bŏnŭs, bŏnă, bŏnŭm, *good.*

	Sing.			Plur.	
Masc.	Fem.	Neut.	Masc.	Fem.	Neut.
N. bŏnŭs,	bŏnă,	bŏnŭm.	N. bŏni,	bŏnæ,	bŏnă.
G. bŏnī,	bŏnæ,	bŏnī.	G. bŏn-ōrum,	-ārŭm,	-orŭm.
D. bŏnō,	bŏnæ,	bŏnō.	D. bŏnīs,	bŏnīs,	bŏnīs.
A. bŏnŭm,	bŏnăm,	bŏnŭm.	A. bŏnōs,	bŏnās,	bŏnă.
V. bŏnĕ,	bŏnă,	bŏnŭm.	V. bŏnī,	bŏnæ,	bŏnă.
A. bŏnō,	bŏnă,	bŏnō.	A. bŏnīs,	bŏnīs,	bŏnīs.

EXAMPLES.

Dĭgnus, lætus, grātus, parvus, māgnus, ămīcus.
Sīccus, perfĭdŭs, antīquus, dĕcōrus, ŏpācus.
Sōbrĭus, dĭūtĭnŭs, implŭs, arctŭs, opīmus.

II. Tĕnĕr, tĕnĕră, tĕnĕrŭm, *tender.*

	Sing.			Plur.	
Masc.	Fem.	Neut.	Masc.	Fem.	Neut.
N. tĕnĕr,	tĕnĕra,	tĕnĕrŭm.	N. tĕnĕrī,	tĕnĕræ,	tĕnĕrĕ.
G. tĕnĕrī,	tĕnĕræ,	tĕnĕrī.	G. tĕnĕr-ōrŭm,	-ārŭm,	-ōrŭm.
D. tĕnĕrō,	tĕnĕræ,	tĕnĕrō.	D. tĕnĕrīs,	tĕnĕrīs,	tĕnĕrīs.
A. tĕnĕrŭm,	tĕnĕrăm,	tĕnĕrŭm.	A. tĕnĕrōs,	tĕnĕrās,	tĕnĕră.
V. tĕnĕr,	tĕnĕră,	tĕnĕrŭm.	V. tĕnĕrī,	tĕnĕræ,	tĕnĕră.
A. tĕnĕrō,	tĕnĕră,	tĕnĕrō.	A. tĕnĕrīs,	tĕnĕrīs,	tĕnĕrīs.

EXAMPLES.

Sĕmĭfĕr, ūxtĕr, prōspĕr, gĭbbĕr, lībĕr, mĭsĕr, ăsper, lacer, and all compounds in fer and ger, as cyprĭfĕr, bĕllĭgĕr, are declined like tĕnĕr; all other Adjectives in ēr of this form lose the e, and are declined like Niger, as follows:

III. Nīgĕr, nīgră, nīgrŭm, *black.*

	Sing.			Plur.	
Masc.	Fem.	Neut.	Masc.	Fem.	Neut.
N. nīgĕr,	nīgră,	nīgrŭm.	N. nīgrī,	nīgræ,	nīgră.
G. nīgrī,	nīgræ,	nīgrī.	G. nīgrōrŭm,	nīgrārŭm,	nīgrōrŭm.
D. nīgrō,	nīgræ,	nīgrō.	D. nīgrīs,	nīgrīs,	nīgrīs.
A. nīgrŭm,	nīgrăm,	nīgrŭm.	A. nīgrōs,	nīgrās,	nīgră.
V. nīgĕr,	nīgră,	nīgrŭm.	V. nīgrī,	nīgræ,	nīgră.
A. nīgrō,	nīgră,	nīgrō.	A. nīgrīs,	nīgrīs,	nīgrīs.

Of one termination :

Fēlīx, *happy.*

	Sing.				Plur.	
Masc.	Fem.	Neut.		Masc.	Fem.	Neut.
N. fēlīx,	fēlīx,	fēlīx.	N. fēlīcēs,	fēlīcēs,	fēlīcĭā.
G. fēlīcĭs,	fēlīcĭs,	fēlīcĭs.	G. fēlīcĭŭm,	-ĭŭm.	-ĭŭm.
D. fēlīcī,	fēlīcī,	fēlīcī.	D. fēlīcĭbŭs,	fēlīcĭbŭs,	-bŭs.
A. fēlīcĕm,	fēlīcĕm,	fēlīx.	A. fēlīcēs,	fēlīcēs,	fēlīcĭā.
V. fēlīx,	fēlīx,	fēlīx.	V. fēlīcēs,	fēlīcēs,	fēlīcĭā.
A. fēlīcĕ,	*or*	fēlīcī.	A. fēlīcĭbŭs,	fēlīcĭbŭs,	-bŭs.

EXAMPLES.

Bĭlix, trĭlix, pērnīx, audax, fĕrōx, sōlērs, vecors, anceps.
Sternax, ămāns, dŏcens, tĕgēns, audĭēns, āmēns, prūdens.

Of two terminations:

Lēnĭs, *mild.*

Masc.	Fem.	Neut.		Masc.	Fem.	Neut.
N. lēnĭs,	lēnĭs,	lēnĕ.	N. lēnēs,	lēnēs,	lēnĭā.
G. lēnĭs,	lēnĭs,	lēnĭs.	G. lēnĭŭm,	lēnĭŭm,	lēnĭŭm.
D. lēni,	lēni,	lēni.	D. lēnĭbŭs,	lēnĭbŭs,	lēnĭbŭs.
A. lēnĕm,	lēnĕm,	lēnĕ.	A. lēnēs,	lēnēs,	lēnĭā.
V. lēnĭs,	lēnĭs,	lēnĕ.	V. lēnēs,	lēnēs,	lēnĭā.
A. lēnī,	lēnī,	lēnī.	A. lēnĭbŭs,	lēnĭbŭs,	lēnĭbŭs.

EXAMPLES.

Utĭlĭs, lĕvĭs, agĭlĭs, mītĭs, civīlĭs, exĭlĭs, hostīlĭs, crudēlĭs.
Sĕnīlĭs, puerīlĭs, juvĕnīlis, vĭrīlis, hĭlāris, lēvĭs, ōmnĭs.

Lĕnĭŏr (the comparative), *milder.*

Masc.	Fem.	Neut.		Masc.	Fem.	Neut.
N. lēnĭŏr,	lēnĭŏr,	lēnĭŭs.	N. lēnĭōrēs,	lēnĭōrēs,	lēnĭōră.
G. lēnĭŏrĭs,	lēnĭŏrĭs,	lēnĭŏrĭs.	G. lēnĭŏr-ŭm,	-ŭm,	-ŭm.
D. lēnĭōrī,	lēnĭōrī,	lēnĭōrī.	D. lēnĭŏrĭ-bŭs, -bŭs,	-bŭs.
A. lēnĭ-ōrĕm, -ōrĕm,	-ŭs.	A. lēnĭōrēs,	lēnĭōrēs,	lēnĭōră.
V. lēnĭŏr,	lēnĭŏr,	lēnĭŭs.	V. lēnĭōrēs,	lēnĭōrēs,	lēnĭōră.
A. lēnĭŏrĕ,	*or*	lēnĭōri.	A. lēnĭŏrĭ-bŭs, -bŭs,	-bŭs.

EXAMPLES.

Mĕlĭŏr, tĕnĕrĭŏr, fēlīcĭŏr, sĕnĭŏr, ācrĭŏr, mĭnōr.
Lĕvior, lēvior, mītĭor, cīvīlĭor, ăgĭlĭor, like lēnĭor.

Prūdens, *prudent.*

Masc. and Fem.	Neut.		Masc. and Fem.	Neut.
N. prūdens.			prūdent-ēs,	prūdent-ĭā.
G. prūdent-ĭs.			prūdent-ĭum.	
D. prūdent-ī.			prūdent-ĭbŭs.	
A. prūdent-em,	prūdens.		prūdent-ēs,	prūdent-ĭā.
V. prūdens.	.		prūdent-ēs,	prūdent-ĭā.
A. prūdent-ī *or* ĕ.			prūdent-ĭbŭs.	

Of three terminations:

Acer, *sharp*.

	Sing.			Plur.	
Masc.	Fem.	Neut.	Masc.	Fem.	Neut.
N. ăcĕr *or* ăcrĭs,	ăcrĭs,	ăcre.	N. ācrēs,	ācrēs,	ăcrĭă.
G. ăcrĭs,	ăcrĭs,	ăcrĭs.	G. ācrĭŭm,	ācrĭŭm,	ācrĭŭm.
D. ăcrī,	ăcrī,	ăcrī.	D. ācrĭbŭs,	ācrĭbŭs,	ācrĭbŭs.
A. ācrĕm,	ācrĕm,	ăcrĕ.	A. ācrēs,	ācrēs,	ăcrĭă.
V. ăcer *or* ăcrĭs,	ăcrĭs,	ăcrĕ.	V. ācrēs,	ācrēs,	ăcrĭă.
A. ăcrī,	ăcrī.	ăcrī.	A. ācrĭbŭs,	ācrĭbŭs,	ācrĭbŭs.

27.   NUMERAL ADJECTIVES.

Arab. Symb.	Roman Symbols.	Cardinals.	Arabic Symbols.	Roman Symbols.	Cardinals.
1	I	ūnus.	23	XXIII	trēs et vīgintī, *or* vīgintī trēs.
2	II	duo.			
3	III	trēs.	28	XXVIII	duŏdētrīgintă.
4	IV	quattuŏr.	29	XXIX	undētrīgintă.
5	V	quinque.	30	XXX	trīgintă.
6	VI	sex.	40	XL	quadrāgintă.
7	VII	septem.	50	L	quinquāgintă.
8	VIII	octo.	60	LX	sexāgintă.
9	IX	nŏvem.	70	LXX	septŭāgintă.
10	X	dĕcem.	80	LXXX	octōgintă.
11	XI	undĕcim.	90	XC	nōnāgintă.
12	XII	duŏdĕcim.	100	C	centum.
13	XIII	trĕdĕcim.	200	CC	dūcenti (ae, ă).
14	XIV	quattuordĕcim.	300	CCC	trēcentī.
15	XV	quindĕcim.	400	CCCC	quadringentī.
16	XVI	sēdĕcim.	500	D, *or* IƆ	quingentī.
17	XVII	septemdĕcim.	600	DC	sexcentī.
18	XVIII	duŏdēvīgintī.	700	DCC	septingentī.
19	XIX	undēvīgintī.	800	DCCC	octingentī.
20	XX	vīgintī.	900	DCCCC	nongentī.
21	XXI	ūnus et vīgintī, *or* vīgintī ūnus.	1000	M, *or* CIƆ	millĕ.
			2000	MM	duŏ milliă.
22	XXII	duŏ et vīgintī, *or* vīgintī duo.	100,000	CCCIƆƆƆ	centum milliă.

28. Of these, unus, duo, and tres are declined irregularly as follows:

Sing.

Masc.	Fem.	Neut.	Masc.	Fem.	Neut.
N. ūn-us,	ūn-a,	ūn-um.	A. ūn-um,	ūn-am,	un-um.
G. ūn-īus.			A. ūn-ō,	ūn-ă,	ūn-ō.
D. ūn-ī.					

The Plural is declined like that of bŏnus.

Singŭlāri caret.		Plur.	Singŭlāri caret.		Plur.
Masc.	Fem.	Neut.	Masc.	Fem.	Neut.
N. dŭo,	dŭæ,	dŭo.	N. trēs,	trēs,	triă.
G. dŭ-ōrŭm,	-ārŭm,	ōrŭm.	G. trĭŭm,	trĭŭm,	trĭŭm.
D. dŭōbŭs	dŭābŭs, dŭōbŭs.		D. trĭbŭs,	trĭbŭs,	trĭbŭs.
A. dŭōs or dŭo,	dŭās,	dŭō.	A. trēs,	trēs,	triă.
V. dŭō,	dŭæ,	dŭō.	V. trēs,	trēs,	triă.
A. dŭōbŭs,	dŭābŭs, dŭōbŭs.		A. trĭbŭs,	trĭbŭs,	trĭbŭs.

From 4 to 100 the Numerals are indeclinable; from 100 to 1000 they are declined like the Plural of bŏnus.

COMPARISON OF ADJECTIVES.

29. Adjectives are compared by adding to the stem of the Positive:

Masc.	Fem.	Neut.
Ior,	Ior,	Ius for the Comparative Degree,
Issimus,	Issima,	Issimum for the Superlative Degree;

as,

Positive.	Comparative.	Superlative.
altus, *high.*	altĭŏr, *higher.*	altissĭmus, *highest, very high.*

IRREGULAR COMPARISON.

30. (*a*) I. Adjectives in er form their Superlative by adding rĭmus to that termination; as, acer, *active;* Genitive, acris; Comparative, acrior; Superlative, acerrĭmus.

In like manner, pauper, pauperrĭmus. Vetus has a similar Superlative, veterrĭmus, as if from veter.

(*b*) Seven Adjectives in lis form their Superlative by adding lĭmus to the root:

facĭlis,	facilĭor,	facillĭmus,	*easy.*
difficĭlis,	difficilĭor,	difficillĭmus,	*difficult.*
gracĭlis,	gracilĭor,	gracillĭmus,	*slender.*
humĭlis,	humilĭor,	humillĭmus,	*low.*
imbecillis,	imbecillĭor,	imbecillĭmus,	*weak.*
simĭlis,	similĭor,	simillĭmus,	*like.*
dissimĭlis,	dissimilĭor,	dissimillĭmus,	*unlike.*

(*c*) Five Adjectives in fĭcus derive their Comparatives and Superlatives from obsolete Adjectives in ens:

B

beneficus,	beneficentior,	beneficentissimus,	*beneficent.*
honorificus,	honorificentior,	honorificentissimus,	*honorable.*
magnificus,	magnificentior,	magnificentissimus,	*splendid.*
munificus,	munificentior,	munificentissimus,	*liberal.*
maleficus,		maleficentissimus,	*hurtful.*

II. The following are compared irregularly :

bŏnus, mĕlior, optĭmus, *good, better, best.*
mălus, pējor, pessimus, *bad, worse, worst.*
magnus, mājŏr, maximus, *great, greater, greatest.*
parvus, mĭnŏr, minĭmus, *small, less, least.*
multum, plūs (n.), plurĭmum, *much, more, most.*
multi, plūres, plurĭmi, *many, more, most.*
nēquam (indecl.), nequĭor, nequissĭmus, *worthless.*
frūgi (indecl.), frugālior, frugalissĭmus, *discreet.*

III. The following are formed from certain Prepositions:

[citra, *this side*] cĭtĕrior, citĭmus, *nearer, nearest.*
[extra, *outside*] extĕrior, extrēmus, *outer, outmost.*
[infra, *below*] infĕrior, infĭmus or īmus, *lower, lowest.*
[intra, *within*] intĕrior, intĭmus, *inner, inmost.*
[post, *after*] postērior, postrēmus or postŭmus, *latter, last.*
[præ, *before*] prĭor, prīmus, *former, first.*
[prŏpe, *near*] proprĭor, proxĭmus, *nearer, next.*
[supra, *above*] sŭpĕrior, suprēmus or summus, *higher, highest.*
[ultra, *beyond*] ultĕrior, ultĭmus, *farther, farthest.*

Juvenis and senex are compared thus, viz. :

juvenus, junior, minimus natu, *young, younger, youngest.*
senex, senior, maximus natu, *old, older, oldest.*

PRONOUNS.

31. Pronouns are
(1.) Personal; viz., ego, tu, and sui (no Nominative).
(2.) Possessive; viz., meus, tuus, suus, noster, and vester.

(3.) Demonstrative; viz., hic, ille, iste, ipse, is, and idem.
(4.) Relative; viz., qui, and its compounds.
(5.) Interrogative; viz., quis and qui.
(6.) Indefinite; viz., quis and qui, and their compounds.
32. They are declined as follows:

I. PERSONAL PRONOUNS.

1. Pronoun of the First Person.

	Sing.		Plur.	
N.	ĕgŏ, *I.*	nŏs,	*we.*
G.	meī, *of me.*	nostrī *and* nostrum, *of us.*
D.	mĭhĭ, *to or for me.*	nōbĭs, *to or for us.*
A.	mē, *me.*	nŏs, *us.* [*from us.*
A.	mē, *by, with,* or *from me.*	nōbĭs, *by, with,* or

2. Pronoun of the Second Person.

	Sing.		Plur.	
N.	tū, *thou.*	vŏs,	*ye or you.*
G.	tuī, *of thee.*	vestrī *and* vestrum, *of you.*
D.	tĭbĭ, *to or for thee.*	vōbĭs, *to or for you.*
A.	tē, *thee.*	vŏs, *you.*
V.	tū, *O thou.*	vŏs, *O ye.* [*you.*
A.	tē, *by, with,* or *from thee.*	vōbĭs, *by, with,* or *from*

II. REFLECTIVE PRONOUN OF THE THIRD PERSON.

	Sing.		Plur.	
G.	suī,	*of himself, herself, itself.*	suī,	*of themselves.*
D.	sĭbĭ,	*to or for himself, herself, itself.*	sĭbĭ,	*to or for themselves.*
A.	sē *or* sĕsē,	*himself, herself, itself.*	sĕ *or* sĕsĕ,	*themselves.*
A.	sē *or* sĕsē,	*by or from himself, herself, itself.*	sĕ *or* sĕsĕ,	*by, from,* or *with themselves.*

33. ### III. POSSESSIVE PRONOUNS.

	Sing.			Plur.		
	Masc.	Fem.	Neut.	Masc.	Fem.	Neut.
N.	meus,	mea,	meum,	mei,	meae,	mea,
G.	mei,	meae,	mei,	meorum,	mearum,	meorum,
D.	meo,	meae,	meo,	meis,	meis,	meis,
A.	meum,	meam,	meum,	meos,	meas,	mea,
V.	mi,	mea,	meum,	mei,	mea,	meas,
A.	meo,	mea,	meo.	meis,	meis,	meis.

So, noster,   nostra,   nostrum,
nostri,   nostrae,   nostri, etc.

34.   IV. DEMONSTRATIVE PRONOUNS.

1. Hic, haec, hoc, *this* (*near me*), *this of mine*.

| | Sing. | | | Plur. | |
Masc.	Fem.	Neut.	Masc.	Fem.	Neut.
N. hic,	haec,	hoc,	hī,	hae,	haec,
G. hūjus,			hōrum,	hārum,	hōrum,
D. huïc,			hīs,		
A. hunc,	hanc,	hoc,	hōs,	hās,	haec,
A. hōc,	hāc,	hōc.	hīs.		

2. Istĕ, istă, istŭd, *that* (*near you*), *that of yours*.

| | Sing. | | | Plur. | |
N.					
N. istĕ,	istă,	istŭd,	istī,	istae,	istă,
G. istïus,			istōrum,	istārum,	istōrum,
D. istī,			istīs,		
A. istum,	istam,	istŭd,	istōs,	istās,	istă,
A. istō,	istā,	istō.	istīs.		

3. Illĕ, illă, illŭd, *that near him, that yonder*.

	Sing.			Plur.	
N. illĕ,	illă,	illŭd,	illī,	illae,	illă,
G. illïus,			illōrum,	illārum,	illōrum,
D. illī,			illīs,		
A. illum,	illam,	illŭd,	illōs,	illās,	illă,
A. illō,	illă,	illō.	illīs.		

Ĭs, ĕa, ĭd, *that*.

	Sing.			Plur.	
N. Ĭs,	eă,	ĭd,	iī,	eae,	eă,
G. ējus,	.		eōrum,	eārum,	eōrum,
D. eï,			iīs *or* eīs,		
A. eum,	eam,	ĭd,	eōs,	eās,	eă,
A. eō,	eā,	eō.	iīs *or* eīs.		

Īdem, eădem, ĭdem, *the same*.

	Sing.			Plur.	
N. īdem,	eădem,	ĭdem,	iīdem,	eaedem,	eădem,
G. ējusdem,			eōrundem,	eārundem,	eōrundem,
D. eīdem,			iīsdem *or* eisdem,		
A. eundem,	eandem,	ĭdem,	eōsdem,	eāsdem,	eădem,
A. eōdem,	eădem,	eōdem.	iīsdem *or* eisdem.		

Ipsĕ, ipsă, ipsum, *self, same.*

	Sing.			Plur.	
	Masc.	Fem.	Neut.	Masc.	Fem.	Neut.
N.	ipsĕ,	ipsă,	ipsum,	ipsi,	ipsae,	ipsă,
G.	ipsīus,			ipsōrum,	ipsārum,	ipsōrum,
D.	ipsī,			ipsīs,		
A.	ipsum,	ipsam,	ipsum,	ipsōs,	ipsās,	ipsă,
A.	ipsō,	ipsă,	ipsō.	ipsīs.		

35. Relative—quī, quae, quŏd, *who* or *which.*

	Sing.			Plur.	
N.	quī,	quae,	quŏd,	quī,	quae,	quae,
G.	cūjus,			quōrum,	quārum,	quōrum,
D.	cuī,			quībus,		
A.	quem,	quam,	quŏd,	quōs,	quās,	quae,
A.	quŏ,	quă,	quŏ.	quībus.		

36. Interrogative—quĭs or quī, quae, quĭd or quŏd, *who? which? what?*

	Sing.			Plur.	
N.	quĭs *or* quī,	quae,	quĭd	quī,	quae,	quae,
G.	cūjus,		[*or* quŏd,	quōrum,	quārum,	quōrum,
D.	cuī,			quībus,		
A.	quem,	quam,	quĭd,	quōs,	quās, .	quae,
A.	quŏ,	quă,	quŏ.	quībus.		

In like manner decline alĭquis, *some one.*

THE VERB.

37. Latin Verbs are
Transitive, which require an object to make complete sense; as, Amo te, *I love thee;* or
Intransitive, which do *not* require such an object; as, Equus currit, *the horse runs.*

VOICES.

38. There are two Voices, the Active and the Passive.
The Active Voice represents the agent as acting upon the object; as, Verbero te, *I strike thee.*
The Passive Voice represents the agent as being acted

upon by some person or thing; as, Virtus laudatur, *virtue is praised.*

MOODS.

39. There are four Moods, viz., tho Indicative, the Subjunctive, the Imperative, and the Infinitive.

The Indicative represents that which actually is or occurs; as, Amo, *I love.*

The Subjunctive represents a possibility or a conception of the mind; as, Amem, *I may love.*

The Imperative represents a command, an exhortation, or an entreaty; as, Ama, *love thou.*

The Infinitive represents simply the meaning of tho Verb, without limitation of person or number; as, Amare, *to love.*

Besides these four Moods, a complete Verb has a Gerund, which is a verbal Noun; four Participles—Present Active, Future Active, Perfect Passive, and Future Passive; and two Supines—the former in um, the latter in u.

TENSES.

40. There are six Tenses, viz. :

The Present, which represents an action as now taking place; as, Amo, *I love.*

The Imperfect, which represents an action which *was* taking place and was not completed in some *past* time; as, Amabam, *I was loving.*

The Future, which represents an action which *will* take place in some future time; as, Amabo, *I shall love.*

The Perfect, which represents an action as either just completed, or as completed in some undetermined *past* time; as, Amavi, *I have loved,* or *I loved.*

The Pluperfect, which represents an action as complete at some past time; as, Amavĕram, *I had loved.*

The Future Perfect, which represents an action which will be completed at or before the completion of some other future action; as, Amavero, *I shall have loved.*

NUMBERS.

41. There are two Numbers, Singular and Plural.

PERSONS.

42. There are three Persons, First, Second, and Third.

CONJUGATION.

43. The regular Latin Verbs are varied in four different ways, called respectively the

First Conjugation, which has A long before RE of the Present Infinitive; as, Amāre.

Second Conjugation, which has E long before RE of the Present Infinitive; as, Delēre.

. Third Conjugation, which has E short before RE of the Present Infinitive; as, Regĕre.

Fourth Conjugation, which has I long before RE of the Present Infinitive; as, Audīre.

44. The Present Indicative Active;

The Present Infinitive Active;

The Perfect Indicative Active; and

The Supine in um,

are called the Principal Parts of the Verb, and to give all four is to *Conjugate the Verb;* thus the following Verbs are conjugated, as below, viz.:

		Present Indicative.	Present Infinitive.	Perfect Indicative.	Supine.
1st	Conj.	amo,	amāre,	amāvi,	amātum.
2d	"	moneo,	monēre,	monŭi,	monĭtum.
"	"	deleo,	delēre,	delēvi,	delētum.
3d	"	rego,	regĕre,	rexi,	rectum.
"	"	capio,	capĕre,	cēpi,	captum.
4th	"	audio,	audīre,	audīvi,	audītum.

THE STEM.

45. The Stem of a Verb is that part which remains unchanged throughout all of the inflections. The Stem is found by dropping the Infinitive Endings, viz.:

āre, in the 1st Conjugation.
ĕre,   "   2d   "
ĕre,   "   3d   "
īre,   "   4th   "

All of the Tenses of a Verb may be formed by adding the proper terminations to this Stem.

46.   **PRINCIPAL PARTS.**

Pres. Ind.	Pres. Inf.	Perf. Ind.
sŭm.	essĕ.	fuī.

INDICATIVE MOOD.

Present Tense. *I am.*

Sing.		Plur.	
sŭm,	*I am.*	sŭmŭs,	*we are.*
ĕs,	*thou art.*	estĭs,	*you are.*
est,	*he is.*	sunt,	*they are.*

Imperfect. *I was.*

ĕrăm,	*I was.*	ĕrămŭs,	*we were.*
ĕrăs,	*thou wast.*	ĕrătĭs,	*you were.*
ĕrăt,	*he was.*	erant,	*they were.*

Future. *I shall or will be.*

ĕrŏ,	*I shall be.*	ĕrĭmŭs,	*we shall be.*
erĭs,	*thou wilt be.*	erĭtĭs,	*you will be.*
erĭt,	*he will be.*	erunt,	*they will be.*

Perfect. *I have been, was.*

fuī,	*I have been.*	fuĭmŭs,	*we have been.*
fuistī,	*thou hast been.*	fuistĭs,	*you have been.*
fuĭt,	*he has been.*	fuĕrunt, fuĕrĕ, }	*they have been.*

Pluperfect. *I had been.*

fuĕrăm,	*I had been.*	fuĕrămŭs,	*we had been.*
fuĕrăs,	*thou hadst been.*	fuĕrătĭs,	*you had been.*
fuĕrăt,	*he had been.*	fuĕrant,	*they had been.*

Future Perfect. *I shall or will have been.*

fuĕrŏ,	*I shall have been.*	fuĕrĭmŭs,	*we shall have been.*
fuĕrĭs,	*thou wilt have been.*	fuĕrĭtĭs,	*you will have been.*
fuĕrĭt,	*he will have been.*	fuĕrint,	*they will have been.*

SUBJUNCTIVE MOOD.

Present. *I may or can be.*

Sing.		Plur.	
sĭm,	*I may be.*	sĭmŭs,	*we may be.*
sĭs,	*thou mayst be.*	sĭtĭs,	*you may be.*
sĭt,	*he may be.*	sĭnt,	*they may be.*

Imperfect. *I might, could, would, or should be.*

essĕm,	*I might be.*	essēmŭs,	*we might be.*
essēs,	*thou mightst be.*	essētĭs,	*you might be.*
essĕt,	*he might be.*	essent,	*they might be.*

Perfect. *I may or can have been.*

fŭĕrĭm,	*I may have been.*	fŭĕrĭmŭs,	*we may have been.*
fŭĕrĭs,	*thou mayst have been.*	fŭĕrĭtĭs,	*you may have been.*
fŭĕrĭt,	*he may have been.*	fŭĕrint,	*they may have been.*

Pluperfect. *I might, could, would, or should have been.*

fuĭssĕm,	*I might have been.*	fuĭssēmŭs,	*we might have been.*
fuĭssēs,	*thou mightst have been.*	fuĭssētĭs,	*you might have been.*
fuĭssĕt,	*he might have been.*	fuĭssent,	*they might have been.*

IMPERATIVE MOOD.

Pres.	ĕs,	*be thou.*	estŏ,	*be ye.*
Fut.	estŏ,	*thou shalt be.*	estōtĕ,	*ye shall be.*
	estŏ,	*he shall be.*	suntŏ,	*they shall be.*

INFINITIVE MOOD.　　　　　PARTICIPLE.

Pres.	essĕ,	*to be.*		
Perf.	fuissĕ,	*to have been.*		
Fut.	fŭtūrŭs essĕ,	*to be about to be.*	Fut. fŭtūrŭs,	*about to be.*

FIRST CONJUGATION.

ACTIVE VOICE.

47. Amo, *I love.*

PRINCIPAL PARTS.

Pres. Ind.	Pres. Inf.	Perf. Ind.	Supine.
ămŏ.	ămārĕ.	ămāvī.	ămātŭm.

INDICATIVE MOOD.

Present Tense. *I love, am loving, do love.*

ămŏ,	*I love.*	ămāmŭs,	*we love.*
ămās,	*thou lovest.*	ămātĭs,	*you love.*
ămăt,	*he loves.*	ămant,	*they love.*

B 2

Imperfect. *I loved, was loving, did love.*
Sing. | **Plur.**

āmābǎm,	I was loving.	āmābāmŭs,	we were loving.
āmābās,	thou wast loving.	āmābātĭs,	you were loving.
āmābǎt,	he was loving.	āmābant,	they were loving.

Future. *I shall or will love.*
āmābǒ,	I shall love.	āmābĭmŭs,	we shall love.
āmābĭs,	thou wilt love.	āmābĭtĭs,	you will love.
āmābĭt,	he will love.	āmābunt,	they will love.

Perfect. *I loved, have loved.*
āmāvī,	I have loved.	āmāvĭmŭs,	we have loved.
āmāvistī,	thou hast loved.	āmāvistĭs,	you have loved.
āmāvĭt,	he has loved.	āmāvērunt, ērē,	they have loved.

Pluperfect. *I had loved.*
āmāvěrǎm,	I had loved.	āmāvěrāmŭs,	we had loved.
āmāvěrās,	thou hadst loved.	āmāvěrātĭs,	you had loved.
āmāvěrǎt,	he had loved.	āmāvěrant,	they had loved.

Future Perfect. *I shall or will have loved.*
āmāvěrǒ,	I shall have loved.	āmāvěrĭmŭs,	we shall have loved.
āmāvěrĭs,	thou wilt have loved.	āmāvěrĭtĭs,	you will have loved.
āmāvěrĭt,	he will have loved.	āmāvěrint,	they will have loved.

SUBJUNCTIVE MOOD.
Present. *I may or can love.*
āměm,	I may love.	āmēmŭs,	we may love.
āmēs,	thou mayst love.	āmētĭs,	you may love.
āmět,	he may love.	āment,	they may love.

Imperfect. *I might, could, would, or should love.*
āmārěm,	I might love.	āmārēmŭs,	we might love.
āmārēs,	thou mightst love.	āmārētĭs,	you might love.
āmārět,	he might love.	āmārent,	they might love.

Perfect. *I may or can have loved.*
āmāvěrĭm,	I may have loved.	āmāvěrĭmŭs,	we may have loved.
āmāvěrĭs,	thou mayst have loved.	āmāvěrĭtĭs,	you may have loved.
āmāvěrĭt,	he may have loved.	āmāvěrint,	they may have loved.

Pluperfect. *I might, could, would, or should have loved.*
āmāvissěm,	I might have loved.	āmāvissēmŭs,	we might have loved.
āmāvissēs,	thou mightst have loved.	āmāvissētĭs,	you might have loved.
āmāvissět,	he might have loved.	āmāvissent,	they might have loved.

IMPERATIVE MOOD.

Sing.		Plur.	
Pres. ămă,	love thou.	ămătŏ,	love ye.
Fut. ămătŏ,	thou shalt love.	ămătŏtŏ,	ye shall love.
ămătŏ,	he shall love.	ămantŏ,	they shall love.

INFINITIVE MOOD.		PARTICIPLE.	
Pres. ămărĕ,	to love.	Pres. ămans,	loving.
Perf. ămăvissĕ,	to have loved.		
Fut. ămātūrŭs estĕ,	to be about to love.	Fut. ămātūrŭs,	about to love.

GERUND.		SUPINE.	
G. ămandī,	of loving.		
D. ămandŏ,	for loving.		
A. ămandŭm,	loving.	A. ămātŭm,	to love.
A. ămandŏ,	by loving.	A. ămătŭ,	to love, be loved.

PASSIVE VOICE.

Amor, I am loved.

PRINCIPAL PARTS.

Pres. Ind.	Pres. Inf.	Perf. Ind.
ămŏr.	ămărī.	ămātŭs sŭm.

INDICATIVE MOOD.

Present Tense. I am loved.

ămŏr,	ămămŭr,
ămărĭs, or rĕ,	ămămĭnī,
ămătŭr.	ămantŭr.

Imperfect. I was loved.

ămăbăr,	ămăbămŭr,
ămăbărĭs, or rĕ,	ămăbămĭnī,
ămăbătŭr.	ămăbantŭr.

Future. I shall or will be loved.

ămăbŏr,	ămăbĭmŭr,
ămăbĕrĭs, or rĕ,	ămăbĭmĭnī,
ămăbĭtŭr.	ămăbuntŭr.

Perfect. I have been or was loved.

ămātŭs sŭm,	ămātī sŭmŭs,
ămātŭs ĕs,	ămātī estĭs,
ămātŭs est.	ămātī sunt.

Pluperfect. *I had been loved.*

Sing.	Plur.
ămātŭs ĕrăm,	ămātī ĕrămŭs,
ămātŭs ĕrăs,	ămātī ĕrătĭs,
ămātŭs ĕrăt.	ămātī ĕrant.

Future Perfect. *I shall or will have been loved.*

ămātŭs ĕrŏ,	ămātī ĕrĭmŭs,
ămātŭs ĕrĭs,	ămātī ĕrĭtĭs,
ămātŭs ĕrĭt.	ămātī ĕrunt.

SUBJUNCTIVE MOOD.

Present. *I may or can be loved.*

ămĕr,	ămēmŭr,
ămērĭs, *or* rĕ,	ămēmĭnĭ,
ămētŭr.	ămentŭr.

Imperfect. *I might, could, would, or should be loved.*

ămārĕr,	ămārēmŭr,
ămārērĭs, *or* rĕ,	ămārēmĭnĭ,
ămārētŭr.	ămārentŭr.

Perfect. *I may have been loved.*

ămātŭs sĭm,	ămātī sīmŭs,
ămātŭs sīs,	ămātī sītĭs,
ămātŭs sĭt.	ămātī sint.

Pluperfect. *I might, could, would, or should have been loved.*

ămātŭs essĕm,	ămātī essēmŭs,
ămātŭs essĕs,	ămātī essētĭs,
ămātŭs essĕt.	ămātī essent.

IMPERATIVE MOOD.

Pres. ămārĕ, *be thou loved.*	ămāmĭnĭ, *be ye loved.*
Fut. ămātŏr, *thou shalt be loved.*	
ămātŏr, *he shall be loved.*	ămantŏr, *they shall be loved.*

INFINITIVE MOOD.   PARTICIPLE.

Pres. ămārī, *to be loved.*	
Perf. ămātŭs essĕ, *to have been loved.*	Perf. ămātŭs, *having been loved.*
Fut. ămātŭm īrī, *to be about to be loved.*	Fut. ămandŭs, *to be loved.*

SECOND CONJUGATION.

ACTIVE VOICE.

48. Moneo, *I advise.*

PRINCIPAL PARTS.

Pres. Ind.	Pres. Inf.	Perf. Ind.	Supine.
mŏneŏ.	mŏnērĕ.	mŏnuī.	mŏnĭtŭm.

INDICATIVE MOOD.

Present Tense. *I advise.*

Sing.	Plur.
mŏneŏ,	mŏnēmŭs,
mŏnēs,	mŏnētĭs,
mŏnĕt.	mŏnent.

Imperfect. *I was advising.*

mŏnēbăm,	mŏnēbāmŭs,
mŏnēbās,	mŏnēbātĭs,
mŏnēbăt.	mŏnēbant.

Future. *I shall or will advise.*

mŏnēbŏ,	mŏnēbĭmŭs,
mŏnēbĭs,	mŏnēbĭtĭs,
mŏnēbĭt.	mŏnēbunt.

Perfect. *I advised or have advised.*

mŏnuī,	mŏnuĭmŭs,
mŏnuistī,	mŏnuistĭs,
mŏnuĭt.	mŏnuērunt, *or* ērĕ.

Pluperfect. *I had advised.*

mŏnuĕrăm,	mŏnuĕrāmŭs,
mŏnuĕrās,	mŏnuĕrātĭs,
mŏnuĕrāt.	mŏnuĕrant.

Future Perfect. *I shall or will have advised.*

mŏnuĕrŏ,	mŏnuĕrĭmŭs,
mŏnuĕrĭs,	mŏnuĕrĭtĭs,
mŏnuĕrĭt.	mŏnuĕrint.

SUBJUNCTIVE MOOD.

Present. *I may or can advise.*

mŏneăm,	mŏneāmŭs,
mŏneās,	mŏneātĭs,
mŏneăt.	mŏneant.

Imperfect. *I might, could, would,* or *should advise.*

Sing.	Plur.
mŏnērēm,	mŏnērēmŭs,
mŏnērēs,	mŏnērētĭs,
mŏnērēt.	mŏnērent.

Perfect. *I may have advised.*

mŏnuĕrĭm,	mŏnuĕrĭmŭs,
mŏnuĕrĭs,	mŏnuĕrĭtĭs,
mŏnuĕrĭt.	mŏnuĕrint.

Pluperfect. *I might, could, would,* or *should have advised.*

mŏnuissēm,	mŏnuissēmŭs,
mŏnuissēs,	mŏnuissētĭs,
mŏnuissēt.	mŏnuissent.

IMPERATIVE MOOD.

Pres.	mŏnē, *advise thou.*	mŏnētē, *advise ye.*
Fut.	mŏnētŏ, *thou shalt advise.*	mŏnētōtŏ, *ye shall advise.*
	mŏnētŏ, *he shall advise.*	mŏnentŏ, *they shall advise.*

INFINITIVE MOOD.

Pres. mŏnēre, *to advise.*
Perf. mŏnuissē, *to have advised.*
Fut. mŏnĭtūrŭs essĕ, *to be about to advise.*

PARTICIPLE.

Pres. mŏnens, *advising.*

Fut. mŏnĭtūrŭs, *about to advise.*

GERUND.

G. mŏnendī,   *of advising.*
D. mŏnendŏ,   *for advising.*
A. mŏnendŭm, *advising.*
A. mŏnendŏ,   *by advising.*

SUPINE.

A. mŏnĭtŭm, *to advise.*
A. mŏnĭtū, *to advise, be advised.*

PASSIVE VOICE.
Moneor, *I am advised.*

PRINCIPAL PARTS.

Pres. Ind.	Pres. Inf.	Perf. Ind.
mŏneŏr.	mŏnērī.	mŏnĭtŭs sŭm.

INDICATIVE MOOD.
Present Tense. *I am advised.*

mŏneŏr,	mŏnēmŭr,
mŏnērĭs, *or* rĕ,	mŏnēmĭnī,
mŏnētŭr.	mŏnentŭr.

Imperfect. *I was advised.*

Sing.	Plur.
mŏnēbăr,	mŏnēbămŭr,
mŏnēbārĭs, *or* rē,	mŏnēbămĭnĭ,
mŏnēbătŭr.	mŏnēbantŭr.

Future. *I shall or will be advised.*

mŏnēbŏr,	mŏnēbĭmŭr,
mŏnēbĕrĭs, *or* rē,	mŏnēbĭmĭnĭ,
mŏnēbĭtŭr.	mŏnēbuntŭr.

Perfect. *I have been or was advised.*

mŏnĭtŭs sŭm,	mŏnĭtĭ sŭmŭs,
mŏnĭtŭs ĕs,	mŏnĭtĭ estĭs,
mŏnĭtŭs est.	mŏnĭtĭ sunt.

Pluperfect. *I had been advised.*

mŏnĭtŭs ĕrăm,	mŏnĭtĭ ĕrămŭs,
mŏnĭtŭs ĕrăs,	mŏnĭtĭ ĕrātĭs,
mŏnĭtŭs ĕrăt.	mŏnĭtĭ ĕrant.

Future Perfect. *I shall or will have been advised.*

mŏnĭtŭs ĕrŏ,	mŏnĭtĭ ĕrĭmŭs,
mŏnĭtŭs ĕrĭs,	mŏnĭtĭ ĕrĭtĭs,
mŏnĭtŭs ĕrĭt.	mŏnĭtĭ ĕrunt.

SUBJUNCTIVE MOOD.

Present. *I may or can be advised.* ·

mŏneăr,	mŏneămŭr,
mŏneārĭs, *or* rē,	mŏneămĭnĭ,
mŏneātŭr.	mŏneantŭr.

Imperfect. *I might, could, would, or should be advised.*

mŏnērĕr,	mŏnērĕmŭr,
mŏnērērĭs, *ór* rē,	mŏnērĕmĭnĭ,
mŏnērētŭr.	mŏnērentŭr.

Perfect. *I may have been advised.*

mŏnĭtŭs sĭm,	mŏnĭtĭ sīmŭs,
mŏnĭtŭs sĭs,	mŏnĭtĭ sītĭs,
mŏnĭtŭs sĭt.	mŏnĭtĭ sint.

Pluperfect. *I might, could, would, or should have been advised.*

mŏnĭtŭs essĕm,	mŏnĭtĭ essēmŭs,
mŏnĭtŭs essēs,	mŏnĭtĭ essētĭs,
mŏnĭtŭs essĕt.	mŏnĭtĭ essent.

IMPERATIVE MOOD.

Sing.	Plur.
Pres. mŏnērĕ, *be thou advised.*	mŏnēmĭnī, *be ye advised.*
Fut. mŏnētŏr, *thou shalt be advised.*	
mŏnētŏr, *he shall be advised.*	mŏnentŏr, *they shall be advised.*

INFINITIVE MOOD.   PARTICIPLE.

Pres. mŏnērī,	*to be advised.*	
Perf. mŏnĭtŭs essĕ, *to have been advised.*		Perf. mŏnĭtŭs, *advised.*
Fut. mŏnĭtŭm ĭrī, *to be about to be advised.*		Fut. mŏnendŭs, *to be advised.*

THIRD CONJUGATION.

ACTIVE VOICE.

49.   Rego, *I rule.*

PRINCIPAL PARTS.

Pres. Ind.	Pres. Inf.	Perf. Ind.	Supine.
rĕgŏ.	rĕgĕrĕ.	rexī.	rectŭm.

INDICATIVE MOOD.

Present Tense. *I rule.*

Sing.	Plur.
rĕgŏ,	rĕgĭmŭs,
rĕgĭs,	rĕgĭtĭs,
rĕgĭt.	rĕgunt.

Imperfect. *I was ruling.*

rĕgēbăm,	rĕgēbămŭs,
rĕgēbās,	rĕgēbătĭs,
rĕgēbăt.	rĕgēbant.

Future. *I shall* or *will rule.*

rĕgăm,	rĕgēmŭs,
rĕgēs,	rŏgētĭs,
rĕgĕt.	rĕgent.

Perfect. *I ruled* or *have ruled.*

rexī,	rexĭmŭs,
rexistī,	rexistĭs,
rexĭt.	rexērunt, *or* ērĕ.

Pluperfect. *I had ruled.*

rexĕrăm,	rexĕrămŭs,
rexĕrās,	rexĕrātĭs,
rexĕrăt.	rexĕrant.

Future Perfect. *I shall or will have ruled.*

<table>
<tr><td>Sing.</td><td>Plur.</td></tr>
<tr><td>rexĕrŏ,</td><td>rexĕrĭmŭs,</td></tr>
<tr><td>rexĕrĭs,</td><td>rexĕrĭtĭs,</td></tr>
<tr><td>rexĕrĭt.</td><td>rexĕrint.</td></tr>
</table>

SUBJUNCTIVE MOOD.

Present. *I may or can rule.*

rĕgăm,	rĕgămŭs,
rĕgăs,	rĕgătĭs,
rĕgăt.	rĕgant.

Imperfect. *I might, could, would, or should rule.*

rĕgĕrĕm,	rĕgĕrĕmŭs,
rĕgĕrĕs,	rĕgĕrĕtĭs,
rĕgĕret.	rĕgĕrent.

Perfect. *I may have ruled.*

rexĕrĭm,	rexĕrĭmŭs,
rexĕrĭs,	rexĕrĭtĭs,
rexĕrĭt.	rexĕrint.

Pluperfect. *I might, could, would, or should have ruled.*

rexissĕm,	rexissĕmŭs,
rexissĕs,	rexissĕtĭs,
rexissĕt.	rexissent.

IMPERATIVE MOOD.

Pres.	regĕ, *rule thou.*	rĕgĭtĕ, *rule ye.*
Fut.	rĕgĭtŏ, *thou shalt rule.*	rĕgĭtōtĕ, *ye shall rule.*
	rĕgĭtŏ, *he shall rule.*	rĕguntŏ, *they shall rule.*

INFINITIVE MOOD.   PARTICIPLE.

Pres.	rĕgĕrĕ,	*to rule.*	Pres. rĕgens, *ruling.*
Perf.	rexissĕ,	*to have ruled.*	
Fut.	rectūrŭs essĕ,	*to be about to rule.*	Fut. rectūrŭs, *about to rule.*

GERUND.   SUPINE.

Gen. rĕgendī,	*of ruling.*	
Dat. rĕgendō,	*for ruling.*	
Acc. rĕgendŭm,	*ruling.*	Acc. rectŭm, *to rule.*
Abl. rĕgendō,	*by ruling.*	Abl. rectū, *to rule, be ruled.*

PASSIVE VOICE.

Regor, *I am ruled.*

PRINCIPAL PARTS.

Pres. Ind.	Pres. Inf.	Perf. Ind.
rĕgŏr.	rĕgī.	rectŭs sŭm.

INDICATIVE MOOD.

Present Tense. *I am ruled.*

Sing.	Plur.
rĕgŏr,	rĕgĭmŭr,
rĕgĕrĭs, *or* rē,	rĕgĭmĭnī,
rĕgĭtŭr.	rĕguntŭr.

Imperfect. *I was ruled.*

rĕgēbăr,	rĕgēbămŭr,
rĕgēbārĭs, *or* rē,	rĕgēbămĭnī,
rĕgēbătŭr.	rĕgēbantŭr.

Future. *I shall or will be ruled.*

rĕgăr,	rĕgēmŭr,
rĕgĕrĭs, *or* rē,	rĕgēmĭnī,
rĕgētŭr.	rĕgentŭr.

Perfect. *I have been or was ruled.*

rectŭs sŭm,	rectī sŭmŭs,
rectŭs ĕs,	rectī estĭs,
rectŭs est.	rectī sunt.

Pluperfect. *I had been ruled.*

rectŭs ĕrăm,	rectī ĕrămŭs,
rectŭs ĕrās,	rectī ĕrātĭs,
rectŭs ĕrăt.	rectī ĕrant.

Future Perfect. *I shall or will have been ruled.*

rectŭs ĕrŏ,	rectī ĕrĭmŭs,
rectŭs ĕrĭs,	rectī ĕrĭtĭs,
rectŭs ĕrĭt.	rectī ĕrunt.

SUBJUNCTIVE MOOD.

Present. *I may or can be ruled.*

rĕgăr,	rĕgămŭr,
rĕgārĭs, *or* rē,	rĕgămĭnī,
rĕgātŭr.	rĕgantŭr.

Imperfect. *I might, could, would, or should be ruled.*

Sing.	Plur.
rĕgĕrĕr,	rĕgĕrēmŭr,
rĕgĕrēris, *or* rē,	rĕgĕrēmĭnĭ,
rĕgĕrētŭr.	rĕgĕrentŭr.

Perfect. *I may have been ruled.*

rectŭs sĭm,	rectĭ sĭmŭs,
rectŭs sĭs,	rectĭ sītĭs,
rectŭs sĭt.	rectĭ sint.

Pluperfect. *I might, could, would, or should have been ruled.*

rectŭs essĕm,	rectĭ essēmŭs,
rectŭs essēs,	rectĭ essētĭs,
rectŭs essĕt.	rectĭ essent.

IMPERATIVE MOOD.

Pres. rĕgĕrĕ, *be thou ruled.* rĕgĭmĭnĭ, *be ye ruled.*
Fut. rĕgĭtŏr, *thou shalt be ruled.*
rĕgĭtŏr, *he shall be ruled.* rĕguntŏr, *ye shall be ruled.*

INFINITIVE MOOD.	PARTICIPLE.

Pres. rĕgĭ, *to be ruled.*
Perf. rectŭs essĕ, *to have been ruled.* Perf. rectŭs, *ruled.*
Fut. rectŭm īrĭ, *to be about to be* Fut. rĕgendŭs, *to be ruled.*
ruled.

FOURTH CONJUGATION.

ACTIVE VOICE.

50. ## Audio, *I hear.*

PRINCIPAL PARTS.

Pres. Ind.	Pres. Inf.	Perf. Ind.	Supine.
audiŏ.	audīrĕ.	audīvĭ.	audītŭm.

INDICATIVE MOOD.

Present Tense. *I hear.*

Sing.	Plur.
audiŏ,	audīmŭs,
audĭs,	audītĭs,
audĭt.	audiunt.

Imperfect. *I was hearing.*

audiēbăm,	audiēbămŭs,
audiēbās,	audiēbātĭs,
audiēbăt.	audiēbant.

Future. *I shall or will hear.*

Sing.	Plur.
audiăm,	audiēmŭs,
audiēs,	audiētĭs,
audiĕt.	audient.

Perfect. *I heard or have heard.*

audīvī,	audīvĭmŭs,
audīvistī,	audīvistĭs,
audīvĭt.	audīvērunt, *or* ērĕ.

Pluperfect. *I had heard.*

audīvĕrăm,	audīvĕrămŭ°,
audīvĕrăs,	audīvĕrătĭs,
audīverăt.	audīvĕrant.

Future Perfect. *I shall or will have heard.*

audīvĕrŏ,	audīvĕrĭmŭs,
audīvĕrĭs,	audīvĕrĭtĭs,
audīvĕrĭt.	audīvĕrint.

SUBJUNCTIVE MOOD.

Present. *I may or can hear.*

audiăm,	audiămŭs,
audiās,	audiătĭs,
audiăt.	audiant.

Imperfect. *I might, could, would,* or *should hear.*

audīrĕm,	audīrĕmŭs,
audīrēs,	audīrētĭs,
audīrĕt.	audīrent.

Perfect. *I may have heard.*

audīvĕrĭm,	audīvĕrĭmŭs,
audīvĕrĭs,	audīvĕrĭtĭs,
audīvĕrĭt.	audīvĕrint.

Pluperfect. *I might, could, would,* or *should have heard.*

audīvissĕm,	audīvissēmŭs,
audīvissēs,	audīvissētĭs,
audīvissĕt.	audīvissent.

IMPERATIVE MOOD.

Pres. audī, *hear thou.*	audītŏ, *hear ye.*
Fut. audītŏ, *thou shalt hear.*	audītōtŏ, *ye shall hear.*
audītŏ, *he shall hear.*	audiuntŏ, *they shall hear.*

INFINITIVE MOOD.		PARTICIPLE.	
Pres. audīrĕ,	to hear.	Pres. audiens,	hearing.
Perf. audīvissĕ,	to have heard.		
Fut. audītūrŭs essĕ,	to be about to hear.	Fut. auditūrŭs,	about to hear.

GERUND.		SUPINE.	
Gen. audiendī,	of hearing.		
Dat. audiendŏ,	for hearing.		
Acc. audiendŭm,	hearing.	Acc. audītŭm,	to hear.
Abl. audiendŏ,	by hearing.	Abl. audītū,	to hear, be heard.

PASSIVE VOICE.

Audior, I am heard.

PRINCIPAL PARTS.

Pres. Ind.	Pres. Inf.	Perf. Ind.
audiŏr.	audīrī.	audītŭs sŭm.

INDICATIVE MOOD.

Present Tense. *I am heard.*

Sing.	Plur.
audiŏr,	audīmŭr,
audīrĭs, *or* rĕ,	audīmĭnī,
audītŭr.	audiuntŭr.

Imperfect. *I was heard.*

audiēbăr,	audiēbāmŭr,
audiēbārĭs, *or* rĕ,	audiēbāmĭnī,
audiēbătŭr.	audiēbantŭr.

Future. *I shall or will be heard.*

audiăr,	audiēmŭr,
audiērĭs, *or* rĕ,	audiēmĭnī,
audiētŭr.	audiēntŭr.

Perfect. *I have been heard.*

audītŭs sŭm,	audītī sŭmŭs,
audītŭs ĕs,	audītī estĭs,
audītŭs est.	audītī sunt.

Pluperfect. *I had been heard.*

audītŭs ĕrăm,	audītī ĕrămŭs,
audītŭs ĕrăs,	audītī ĕrătĭs,
audītŭs ĕrăt.	audītī ĕrant.

Future Perfect. *I shall* or *will have been heard.*

Sing.	Plur.
audītŭs ĕrŏ,	audītī ĕrĭmŭs,
audītŭs ĕrĭs,	audītī ĕrĭtĭs,
audītŭs ĕrĭt.	audītī ĕrunt.

SUBJUNCTIVE MOOD.

Present. *I may* or *can be heard.*

audiăr,	audiămŭr,
audiărĭs, *or* rĕ,	audiămĭnī,
audiătŭr.	audiantŭr.

Imperfect. *I might, could, would,* or *should be heard.*

audīrĕr,	audīrēmŭr,
audīrērĭs, *or* rĕ,	audīrēmĭnī,
audīrētŭr.	audīrentŭr.

Perfect. *I may have been heard.*

audītŭs sĭm,	audītī sīmŭs,
audītŭs sĭs,	audītī sītĭs,
audītŭs sĭt.	audītī sint.

Pluperfect. *I might, could, would,* or *should have been heard.*

audītŭs essĕm,	audītī essēmŭs,
audītŭs essēs,	audītī essētĭs,
audītŭs essĕt.	audītī essent.

IMPERATIVE MOOD.

Pres. audīrĕ, *be thou heard.*	audīmĭnī, *be ye heard.*
Fut. audītŏr, *thou shalt be heard.*	
audītŏr, *he shall be heard.*	audiuntŏr, *they shall be heard.*

INFINITIVE MOOD.

Pres. audīrī, *to be heard.*

Perf. audītŭs essĕ, *to have been heard.*

Fut. audītŭm īrī, *to be about to be heard.*

PARTICIPLE.

Perf. audītŭs, *heard.*

Fut. audiendŭs, *to be heard.*

THIRD CONJUGATION (*mixed with the Fourth*).

51. Căpio, căpĕrĕ, cēpī, captum, *to take.*

ACTIVE VOICE.

INDICATIVE MOOD.

Present Tense.

S. căp-io,	*I take.*	P. căp-ĭmŭs,	*we take.*
căp-ĭs,	*thou takest.*	căp-ĭtĭs,	*you take.*
căp-ĭt,	*he takes.*	căp-iunt,	*they take.*

Imperfect Tense.

S. căp-iēbam,	*I was taking.*	P. căp-iēbāmŭs,	*we were taking.*
căp-iēbās,	*thou wast taking.*	căp-iēbātĭs,	*you were taking.*
căp-iēbăt,	*he was taking.*	căp-iēbant,	*they were taking.*

Future Tense.

S. căp-iam,	*I shall take.*	P. căp-iēmŭs,	*we shall take.*
căp-iēs,	*thou wilt take.*	căp-iētĭs,	*you will take.*
căp-iĕt,	*he will take.*	căp-ient,	*they will take.*

Perfect Tense.

| cēp-ī, | *I have taken, or I took,* | like | rexi. |

Pluperfect Tense.

| cēp-ĕram, | *I had taken,* | like | rexĕram. |

Future Perfect Tense.

| cēp-ĕro, | *I shall have taken,* | like | rexĕro. |

SUBJUNCTIVE MOOD.

Present Tense.

S. căp-iam,	*I may take.*	P. căp-iāmŭs,	*we may take.*
căp-iās,	*thou mayst take.*	căp-iātĭs,	*you may take.*
căp-iăt,	*he may take.*	căp-iant,	*they may take.*

Imperfect Tense.

S. căp-ĕrem,	*I might take.*	P. căp-ĕrēmŭs,	*we might take.*
căp-ĕrēs,	*thou mightst take.*	căp-ĕrētĭs,	*you might take.*
căp-ĕrĕt,	*he might take.*	căp-ĕrent,	*they might take.*

Perfect Tense.

| cēp-ĕrim, | *I may have taken,* | like | rexĕrim. |

Pluperfect Tense.

| cēp-issem, | *I might have taken,* | like | rexissem. |

IMPERATIVE MOOD.
Present Tense.

S. **căp-ŏ,**   *take thou.*
   căp-Ĭto, *thou shalt take.*
   căp-Ĭto, *he shall take,* or *let him take.*

P. **căp-Ĭtŏ,**   *take ye or you.*
   căp-Ĭtŏtŏ, *you shall take.*
   căp-iunto, *they shall take,* or *let them take.*

INFINITIVE MOOD.

Pres. **căp-ĕrĕ,**   *to take.*
Perf. **cĕp-isse,**   *to have taken.*
Fut. **cap-tūrum esse,** *to be about to take.*

GERUND.

Gen. **căp-iendi,**   *of taking.*
Dat. **căp-iendo,**   *for taking.*
Acc. **căp-iendum,** *the taking.*
Abl. **căp-iendo,**   *by taking.*

SUPINES.

cap-tum, *to take.*
cap-tu, *to be taken.*

PARTICIPLES.

Pres. **căp-iens,** *taking.*
Fut. **cap-tūrus,** *about to take.*

PASSIVE VOICE.
INDICATIVE MOOD.
Present Tense.

S. **căp-ĭŏr,**   *I am taken.*
   căp-ĕrĭs, *or* **-ĕrĕ,** *thou art taken.*
   căp-ĭtŭr,   *he is taken.*

P. **căp-ĭmŭr,**   *we are taken.*
   căp-ĭmĭnĭ, *you are taken.*
   căp-iuntŭr, *they are taken.*

Imperfect Tense.

S. **căp-iēbar,**   *I was being taken.*
   căp-iēbāris, *or*   *thou wast being*
   cap-iēbāre,   *taken.*
   căp-iēbātŭr,   *he was being taken.*

P. **căp-iēbāmŭr,** *we were being taken.*
   căp-iēbāmĭni, *you were being taken.*
   căp-iēbantŭr, *they were being taken.*

Future Tense.

S. **căp-iar,**   *I shall be taken.*
   căp-iēris, *or*   *thou wilt be*
   căp-iēre,   *taken.*
   căp-iētŭr,   *he will be taken.*

P. **căp-iēmŭr,**   *we shall be taken.*
   căp-iēmĭni, *you will be taken.*
   căp-ientŭr, *they will be taken.*

Perfect Tense.

cap-tus sum, *or* **fui,**   { *I have been taken,* or } like { **rectus sum,** *or* **fui.** }
   { *I was taken,* }

Pluperfect Tense.

cap-tus ĕram, *or* **fuĕram,** *I had been taken.*   like { **rectus ĕram,** *or* **fuĕram.** }

Future Perfect Tense.

cap-tus ĕro, *or* **fuĕro,**   *I shall have been taken,*   like { **rectus ĕro,** *or* **fuĕro.** }

SUBJUNCTIVE MOOD.

Present Tense.

S. căp-iar,   *I may be taken.*   *P.* căp-iămŭr,   *we may be taken.*

căp-iăris, *or*⎫ *thou mayst be*   căp-iămĭni,   *you may be taken.*
cap-iăre, ⎭   *taken.*

cap-iătŭr,   *he may be taken.*   căp-iantŭr,   *they may be taken.*

Imperfect Tense.

S. căp-ĕrer,   *I might be taken.*   *P.* căp-ĕrēmŭr,   *we might be taken.*

căp-ĕrēris, *or*⎫ *thou mightst be*   căp-ĕrēmĭni,   *you might be taken.*
căp-ĕrēre, ⎭   *taken.*

căp-ĕrētur,   *he might be taken.*   căp-ĕrentur,   *they might be*
taken.

Perfect Tense.

cap-tus sim, *or* fuĕrim,   *I may have been taken,*   like ⎰ rectus sim, *or*
⎱ fuĕrim.

Pluperfect Tense.

cap-tus essem, *or* fuissem,   *I might have been taken,*   like ⎰ rectus essem,
⎱ *or* fuissem.

IMPERATIVE MOOD.

Present Tense.

S. căp-ĕrĕ, *be thou taken.*   *P.* căp-ĭmĭni, *be ye* or *you taken.*

căp-ĭtŏr, *thou shalt be taken.*   căp-iuntor, *they shall be taken,*

căp-ĭtŏr, *he shall be taken,* or *let*   or *let them be*
him be taken.   *taken.*

INFINITIVE MOOD.

Pres. căp-ĭ,   *to be taken.*

Perf. cap-tum esse, *or* fuisse,   *to have been taken.*

Fut. cap-tum iri,   *to be about to be taken.*

PARTICIPLES.

Perf. cap-tus (a, um),   *taken,* or *having been taken.*

Ger. căp-iendus (a, um),   *fit to be taken.*

C

DEPONENT

52. A Deponent Verb is that which, under a passive
speak; mŏrior, *I die.*

   I. Hortŏr, hortātŭs sum, hortārī, *to exhort,* like ămŏr.
  II. Vĕreŏr, vĕrĭtŭs sum, vĕrērī, *to fear,* " mŏneŏr.

		I.		II.	
INDICATIVE MOOD.	*Present.*	Hort-ŏr,	*I exhort.*	Vĕr-eŏr,	*I fear.*
		Hort-ārĭs (ărĕ), etc.	} *thou exhortest.* etc.	Vĕr-ērĭs (ĕrĕ), etc.	} *thou fearest.* etc.
	Imperf.	Hort-ābăr,	*I was exhorting.*	Vĕr-ĕbăr,	*I was fearing.*
	Future.	Hort-ābŏr,	*I shall exhort.*	Vĕr-ĕbŏr,	*I shall fear.*
	Perfect.	Hort-ātŭs sum,	} *I have exhorted or I exhorted.*	Vĕr-ĭtŭs sum,	} *I have feared or I feared.*
	Pluperf.	Hort-ātŭs ĕram,	} *I had exhorted.*	Vĕr-ĭtŭs ĕram,	} *I had feared.*
	Fut. Perf.	Hort-ātŭs ĕro,	} *I shall have exhorted.*	Vĕr-ĭtŭs ĕro,	} *I shall have feared.*
SUBJUNCTIVE MOOD.	*Present.*	Hort-ĕr,	*I may exhort.*	Vĕr-eăr,	*I may fear.*
	Imperf.	Hort-ărĕr,	*I might exhort.*	Vĕr-ērĕr,	*I might fear.*
	Perfect.	Hort-ātŭs sim,	} *I may have exhorted.*	Vĕr-ĭtŭs sim,	} *I may have feared.*
	Pluperf.	Hort-ātŭs essem,	} *I might have exhorted.*	Vĕr-ĭtŭs essem,	} *I might have feared.*
IMPERATIVE.	*Present.*	Hort-ārĕ,	*Exhort thou.*	Vĕr-ērĕ,	*Fear thou.*
		Hort-ātŏr,	} *thou shalt exhort.*	Vĕr-ētŏr,	} *thou shalt fear.*
INFINITIVE.	*Present.*	Hort-ārī,	*to exhort.*	Vĕr-ērī,	*to fear.*
	Perfect.	Hort-ātum essĕ,	} *to have exhorted.*	Vĕr-ĭtum essĕ,	} *to have feared.*
	Future.	Hort-ātūrum essĕ,	} *to be about to exhort.*	Vĕr-ĭtŭrum essĕ,	} *to be about to fear.*
PARTICIPLES.	*Present.*	Hort-ans,	*exhorting.*	Vĕr-ens,	*fearing.*
	Future.	Hort-ātūrŭs,	*about to exhort.*	Vĕr-ĭtūrŭs,	*about to fear.*
	Perfect.	Hort-ātŭs,	*having exhorted.*	Vĕr-ĭtŭs,	*having feared.*
	Gerundive.	Hort-andŭs,	{ *fit to be exhorted.*	Vĕr-endŭs,	*fit to be feared.*
SUPINES.		Hort-ātum,	*to exhort.*	Vĕr-ĭtum,	*to fear.*
		Hort-ātū,	*to be exhorted.*	Vĕr-ĭtū,	*to be feared.*
GERUND.		Hort-andi, etc.	*of exhorting,* etc.	Vĕr-endi, etc.	*of fearing,* etc.

VERBS.

form, has an active or neuter signification; as, Lŏquor, *I*

III. Lŏquŏr, lŏcūtŭs sum, lŏquī, *to speak,* like rĕgŏr.
IV. Partiŏr, partītŭs sum, partīrī, *to divide,* " audiŏr.

	III.			IV.		
Present.	Lŏqu-ŏr,	*I speak.*	Part-iŏr,	*I divide.*		
	Lŏqu-ĕrĭs (ĕrĕ), etc.	} *thou speakest.*	Part-īrĭs (īrĕ), etc.	} *thou dividest.*		INDICATIVE MOOD.
Imperf.	Lŏqu-ēbăr,	*I was speaking.*	Part-iēbăr,	*I was dividing.*		
Future.	Lŏqu-ăr,	*I shall speak.*	Part-iăr,	*I shall divide.*		
Perfect.	Lŏcū-tŭs sum,	} *I have spoken or I spoke.*	Part-ītŭs sum,	} *I have divided or I divided.*		
Pluperf.	Lŏcū-tŭs ĕram,	} *I had spoken.*	Part-ītŭs ĕram,	} *I had divided.*		
Fut. Perf.	Lŏcū-tŭs ĕro,	} *I shall have spoken.*	Part-ītŭs ĕro,	} *I shall have divided.*		
Present.	Lŏqu-ăr,	*I may speak.*	Part-iăr,	*I may divide.*		
Imperf.	Lŏqu-ĕrĕr,	*I might speak.*	Part-īrĕr,	*I might divide.*		SUBJUNCTIVE MOOD.
Perfect.	Lŏcū-tŭs sim,	} *I may have spoken.*	Part-ītŭs sim,	} *I may have divided.*		
Pluperf.	Lŏcū-tŭs essem,	} *I might have spoken.*	Part-ītŭs essem,	} *I might have divided.*		
Present.	Lŏqu-ĕrĕ,	*Speak thou.*	Part-īrĕ,	*Divide thou.*		IMPERATIVE.
	Lŏqu-ītŏr,	{ *thou shalt speak.*	Part-ītŏr,	} *thou shalt divide.*		
Present.	Lŏqu-ī,	*to speak.*	Part-īrī,	*to divide.*		
Perfect.	Lŏcū-tum essĕ,	} *to have spoken.*	Part-ītum essĕ,	} *to have divided.*		INFINITIVE.
Future.	Lŏcū-tūrum essĕ,	} *to be about to speak.*	Part-ītūrum essĕ,	} *to be about to divide.*		
Present.	Lŏqu-ens,	*speaking.*	Part-iens,	*dividing.*		
Future.	Lŏcū-tūrŭs,	*about to speak.*	Part-ītūrŭs,	*about to divide.*		PARTICIPLES.
Perfect.	Lŏcū-tŭs,	*having spoken.*	Part-ītŭs,	*having divided.*		
Gerundive.	Lŏqu-ĕndŭs,	*fit to be spoken.*	Part-iendŭs,	*fit to be divided.*		
SUPINES.	Lŏcū-tum,	*to speak.*	Part-ītum,	*to divide.*		
	Lŏcū-tū,	*to be spoken.*	Part-ītū,	*to be divided.*		
GERUND.	Lŏqu-endi, etc.	*of speaking, etc.*	Part-iendi, etc.	*of dividing, etc.*		

IRREGULAR VERBS.

53. The following Verbs, with their compounds, are called Irregular Verbs, viz., sum, edo, fero, volo, fio, eo, and queo.

54. Possum, *I am able*, is composed of potis and sum, and is varied as follows:

Possum, pŏtuī, possĕ, *to be able, can.*

INDICATIVE.	SUBJUNCTIVE.	INDICATIVE.	SUBJUNCTIVE.
Present.		*Imperfect.*	
S. pos-sum,	pos-sim.	*S.* pŏt-ĕram,	pos-sem.
pŏt-ĕs,	pos-sīs.	pŏt-ĕrăs,	pos-sēs.
pŏt-est,	pos-sīt.	pŏt-ĕrăt,	pos-sĕt.
P. pos-sŭmŭs,	pos-sīmŭs.	*P.* pŏt-ĕrămŭs,	pos-sēmŭs.
pŏt-estĭs,	pos-sītĭs.	pŏt-ĕrātĭs,	pos-sētĭs.
pos-sunt,	pos-sint.	pŏt-ĕrant,	pos-sent.
Future.		*Pluperfect.*	
S. pŏt-ĕro.	(wanting.)	*S.* pŏt-uĕram,	pŏt-uissem.
pŏt-ĕrĭs.		pŏt-uĕrăs,	pŏt-uissēs.
pŏt-ĕrĭt.		pŏt-uĕrăt,	pŏt-uissĕt.
P. pŏt-ĕrĭmŭs.		*P.* pŏt-uĕrămŭs,	pŏt-uissēmŭs.
pŏt-ĕrĭtĭs.		pŏt-uĕrātĭs,	pŏt-uissētĭs.
pŏt-ĕrunt.		pŏt-uĕrant,	pŏt-uissent.
Perfect.		*Future Perfect.*	
S. pŏt-uī,	pŏt-uĕrim.	*S.* pŏt-uĕro.	(wanting.)
pŏt-uistī,	pŏt-uĕrĭs.	pŏt-uĕrĭs.	
pŏt-uĭt,	pŏt-uĕrĭt.	pŏt-uĕrĭt.	
P. pŏt-uĭmŭs,	pŏt-uĕrimŭs.	*P.* pŏt-uĕrimŭs.	
pŏt-uistĭs,	pŏt-uĕritĭs.	pŏt-uĕritĭs.	
pŏt-uērunt(ĕrĕ),pŏt-uĕrint.		pŏt-uĕrint.	

INFINITIVE MOOD.

Imperfect. possĕ. *Perfect.* pŏtuissĕ. *Future.* (wanting.)

55. Prosum, prodesse, profui.

INDICATIVE MOOD.

Pr.	prō-sum,	prŏd-es, prŏd-est;	prō-sŭmus, prŏd-estis, etc.
Imp.	prŏd-ĕram,	prŏd-ĕras, prŏd-ĕrat;	prŏd-erāmus, etc.
Perf.	prō-fūi,	prō-fuisti, prō-fuit;	prō-fuĭmus, prō-fuistis, etc.
Plu.	prō-fuĕram,	prō-fuĕras, prō-fuĕrat;	prō-fuerāmus, etc.
Fut.	prŏd-ĕro,	prŏd-ĕris, prŏd-ĕrit;	prŏd-erĭmus, etc.
Fut. } *Perf.* }	prō-fuĕro,	prō-fuĕris, prō-fuĕrit;	prō-fuerĭmus, etc.

SUBJUNCTIVE MOOD.

Pr. prō-sim, prō-sis, prō-sit; prō-sīmus, prō-sītis, prō-sint.
Imp. prŏd-essem, prŏd-esses, prŏd-esset; prŏd-essēmus, etc.
Perf. prō-fuĕrim, prō-fuĕris, prō-fuĕrit; prō-fuerĭmus, etc.
Plu. prō-fuissem, prō-fuisses, prō-fuisset; prō-fuissēmus, etc.

IMPERATIVE MOOD.

Pr. prŏd-ĕs *or* prŏd-esto,　　　　　prŏd-estĕ *or* prŏd-estōte,
　　　prŏd-esto,　　　　　　　　　　prō-sunto.

INFINITIVE MOOD.

Pr. prŏd-essĕ.　　　　　　*Fut.* essĕ pro-futūrus, -ă, -ŭm.
Perf. prō-fuissĕ.　　　　　　　　fuisse prō-futūrūs.

PARTICIPLE.

Fut. prō-futūrūs.

Edo, *I eat.*

56. This Verb is sometimes regular, and sometimes takes forms like those of *sum* which begin in *es.* Thus:

　　　edō,　　ĕdĕrĕ,　　ēdī,　　ēsūm.

INDICATIVE MOOD.
Present.

ĕdō,　　ĕdĭs,　　ĕdĭt;　　ĕdĭmŭs,　　ĕdĭtĭs,　　ĕdunt.
　-　ēs,　　est;　　　　　　　　　　estis.

SUBJUNCTIVE MOOD.
Imperfect.

ĕdĕrĕm,　ĕdĕrēs,　ĕdĕrĕt;　ĕdĕrēmŭs,　ĕdĕrētĭs,　ĕdĕrent.
essĕm,　　essēs,　　essĕt;　　essēmŭs,　　essētĭs,　　essent.

IMPERATIVE MOOD.

Present.　　　　　　　　　　　*Future.*
ĕdĕ,　　ĕdĭte.　　　　　　ĕdĭtō;　　ĕdĭtōte,　ĕduntō.
ēs,　　estĕ.　　　　　　estō;　　estōtĕ.

INFINITIVE MOOD.
Present.

ĕdĕrĕ,　　essĕ.

57. Fĕro, tŭlī, ferrĕ, lātum, *to bear, carry, endure.*

I. ACTIVE VOICE.

INDICATIVE.	SUBJUNCTIVE.	INDICATIVE.	SUBJUNCTIVE.
		Present.	
S. fĕr-o,	fĕr-am.	*P.* fĕr-ĭmŭs,	fĕr-āmŭs.
fer-s,	fĕr-ās.	fer-tĭs,	fĕr-ātĭs.
fer-t,	fĕr-ăt.	fĕr-unt,	fĕr-ant.

INDICATIVE.	SUBJUNCTIVE.		INDICATIVE.	SUBJUNCTIVE.
Imperfect.			*Future.*	

S. fĕr-ēbam,   fer-rem.   *S.* fĕr-am,
fĕr-ēbās,   fer-rēs.   fĕr-ēs,
fĕr-ēbāt,   fer-rēt.   fĕr-ĕt.
P. fĕr-ēbāmŭs,   fer-rēmŭs.   *P.* fĕr-ēmŭs,
fĕr-ēbātĭs,   fer-rētĭs.   fĕr-ētĭs,
fĕr-ēbant,   fer-rent.   fĕr-ent.

Perfect.   *Pluperfect.*

S. tŭl-ī,   tŭl-ĕrim.   *S.* tŭl-ĕram,   tŭl-issem.
tŭl-istī,   tŭl-ĕris.   tŭl-ĕrās,   tŭl-issēs.
tŭl-ĭt,   tŭl-ĕrĭt.   tŭl-ĕrāt,   tŭl-issĕt.
P. tŭl-ĭmŭs,   tŭl-ĕrimŭs.   *P.* tŭl-ĕrāmŭs,   tŭl-issēmŭs.
tŭl-istĭs,   tŭl-ĕritĭs.   tŭl-ĕrātĭs,   tŭl-issētĭs.
tŭl-ērunt *or* ērĕ,   tŭl-ĕrint.   tŭl-ĕrant,   tŭl-issent.

Future Perfect.

S. tŭl-ĕro.   (wanting.)   *P.* tŭl-ĕrimŭs.   (wanting.)
tŭl-ĕris.   tŭl-ĕritĭs.
tŭl-ĕrĭt.   tŭl-ĕrint.

IMPERATIVE.   PARTICIPLES.

Present. fĕr,   *Imperfect.* fĕr-ens.
fer-to,   *Future.* lātūrŭs (a, ŭm).
fer-to,
fer-tŏ,   SUPINES.
fer-tōtĕ,   lātum,
fĕr-unto.   lātū.

INFINITIVE.

Imperfect. fer-rĕ.   GERUND.
Perfect. tŭl-issĕ.   *Gen.*   fĕr-endī,
Future. lātūrum essĕ.   etc.

II. PASSIVE VOICE.

INDICATIVE.	SUBJUNCTIVE.		INDICATIVE.	SUBJUNCTIVE.
Present.			*Imperfect.*	

S. fĕr-ŏr,   fĕr-ăr.   *S.* fĕr-ēbăr,   fer-rĕr.
fer-rĭs,   fĕr-ārĭs.   fĕr-ēbārĭs,   fer-rērĭs.
fer-tŭr,   fĕr-ātŭr.   fĕr-ēbātŭr,   fer-rētŭr.
P. fĕr-ĭmŭr,   fĕr-āmŭr.   *P.* fĕr-ēbāmŭr,   fer-rēmŭr.
fĕr-ĭmĭnī,   fĕr-āmĭnī.   fĕr-ēbāmĭnī,   fer-rēmĭnī.
fĕr-untŭr,   fĕr-antŭr.   fĕr-ēbantŭr,   fer-rentŭr.

Future.

S. fĕr-ăr.   (wanting.)   *P.* fĕr-ēmŭr.   (wanting.)
fĕr-ērĭs.   fĕr-ēmĭnī.
fĕr-ētŭr.   fĕr-entŭr.

<table>
<tr><td colspan="2">Perfect.</td><td colspan="2">Pluperfect.</td></tr>
</table>

S. lātŭs sum,	lātŭs sim.	*S.* lātŭs ĕram,	lātŭs essem.
lātŭs ĕs,	lātŭs sīs.	lātŭs ĕrās,	lātŭs essēs.
lātŭs est,	lātŭs sĭt.	lātŭs ĕrăt,	lātŭs essĕt.
P. lātī sŭmus,	lātī sīmŭs.	*P.* lātī ĕrāmŭs,	lātī essēmŭs.
lātī estĭs,	lātī sītĭs.	lātī ĕrātĭs,	lātī essētĭs.
lātī sunt,	lātī sint.	lātī ĕrant,	lāti essent.

Future Perfect.

S. lātŭs ĕro.	(wanting.)	*P.* lātī ĕrĭmŭs.	(wanting.)
lātŭs ĕrĭs.		lātī ĕrĭtĭs.	
lātŭs ĕrĭt.		lātī ĕrunt.	

IMPERATIVE.	INFINITIVE.
Present. fer-rĕ,	*Imperfect.* fer-ri.
fer-tŏr,	*Perfect.* lātum essĕ.
fer-tŏr,	*Future.* lātum īrī.
fĕr-ĭmĭnī,	PARTICIPLES.
fĕr-untŏr.	*Perfect.* lātŭs (a, um).
	Gerundive. fĕr-endŭs (a, um).

58. Vŏlo, vŏluī, vellĕ, *to be willing, to wish.*
Nōlo, nōluī, nolle, *to be unwilling, not to wish.*
Mālo, māluī, mallĕ, *to be more willing, to prefer, to have rather.*

INDICATIVE.
Present.

S. vŏlo,	nōlo,	mālo.
vīs,	nōn vīs,	māvīs.
vult,	nōn vult,	māvult.
P. vŏlŭmŭs,	nōlŭmŭs,	mālŭmŭs.
vultĭs,	nōn vultĭs,	māvultĭs.
vŏlunt,	nōlunt,	mālunt.

Imperfect.

S. vŏl-ēbam,	nōl-ēbam,	māl-ēbam.
vŏl-ēbās,	nōl-ēbās,	māl-ēbās.
vŏl-ēbăt,	nōl-ēbăt,	māl-ēbăt.
P. vŏl-ēbāmŭs,	nōl-ēbāmŭs,	māl-ēbāmŭs.
vŏl-ēbātĭs,	nōl-ēbātĭs,	māl-ēbātĭs.
vŏl-ēbant,	nōl-ēbant,	māl-ēbant.

Future.

S. vŏl-am,	nōl-am,	māl-am.
vŏl-ēs,	nōl-ēs,	māl-ēs.
vŏl-ĕt,	nōl-ĕt,	māl-ĕt.

Future.

P. vŏl-ēmŭs,	nōl-ēmŭs,	māl-ēmŭs.
vŏl-ētĭs,	nōl-ētĭs,	māl-ētĭs.
vŏl-ent,	nōl-ent,	māl-ent.

Perfect.

S. vŏl-uī,	nōl-uī,	māl-uī.
vŏl-uistī,	nōl-uistī,	māl-uistī.
vŏl-uĭt,	nōl-uĭt,	māl-uĭt.
P. vŏl-uĭmŭs,	nōl-uĭmŭs,	māl-uĭmŭs.
vŏl-uistĭs,	nōl-uistĭs,	māl-uistĭs.
vŏl-uērunt or -uērĕ,	nōl-uērunt or -uērĕ,	māl-uērunt or -uērĕ.

Pluperfect.

S. vŏl-uĕram,	nōl-uĕram,	māl-uĕram.
vŏl-uĕrās,	nōl-uĕrās,	māl-uĕrās.
vŏl-uĕrăt,	nōl-uĕrăt,	māl-uĕrăt.
P. vŏl-uĕrāmŭs,	nōl-uĕrāmŭs,	māl-uĕrāmŭs.
vŏl-uĕrātĭs,	nōl-uĕrātĭs,	māl-uĕrātĭs.
vŏl-uĕrant,	nōl-uĕrant,	māl-uĕrant.

Future Perfect.

S. vŏl-uĕro,	nōl-uĕro,	māl-uĕro.
vŏl-uĕris,	nōl-uĕris,	māl-uĕris.
vŏl-uĕrĭt,	nōl-uĕrĭt,	māl uĕrĭt.
P. vŏl-uĕrimŭs,	nōl-uĕrimŭs,	māl-uĕrimŭs.
vŏl-uĕritĭs,	nōl-uĕritĭs,	māl-uĕritĭs.
vŏl-uĕrint,	nōl-uĕrint,	māl-uĕrint.

SUBJUNCTIVE.
Present.

S. vĕl-im,	nōl-im,	māl-im.
vĕl-īs,	nōl-īs,	māl-īs.
vĕl-ĭt,	nōl-ĭt,	māl-ĭt.
P. vĕl-īmŭs,	nōl-īmŭs,	māl-īmŭs.
vĕl-ītĭs,	nōl-ītĭs,	māl-ītĭs.
vĕl-int,	nōl-int,	māl-int.

Imperfect.

S. vel-lem,	nol-lem,	mal-lem.
vel-lēs,	nol-lēs,	mal-lēs.
vel-lĕt,	nol-lĕt,	mal-lĕt.
P. vel-lēmŭs,	nol-lēmŭs,	mal-lēmŭs.
vel-lētĭs,	nol-lētĭs,	mal-lētĭs.
vel-lent,	nol-lent,	mal-lent.

Perfect.

S. vŏl-ŭĕrim,	nŏl-ŭĕrim,	măl-ŭĕrim.
vŏl-ŭĕris,	nŏl-ŭĕris,	măl-ŭĕris.
vŏl-ŭĕrĭt,	nŏl-ŭĕrĭt,	măl-ŭĕrĭt.
P. vŏl-ŭĕrimŭs,	nŏl-ŭĕrimŭs,	măl-ŭĕrimŭs.
vŏl-ŭĕritĭs,	nŏl-ŭĕritĭs,	măl-ŭĕritĭs.
vŏl-ŭĕrint,	nŏl-ŭĕrint,	măl-ŭĕrint.

Pluperfect.

S. vŏl-uissem,	nŏl-uissem,	măl-uissem.
vŏl-uissēs,	nŏl-uissēs,	măl-uissēs.
vŏl-uissĕt,	nŏl-uissĕt,	măl-uissĕt.
P. vŏl-uissēmŭs,	nŏl-uissēmŭs,	măl-uissēmŭs.
vŏl-uissētĭs,	nŏl uissētĭs,	măl-uĭssētĭs.
vŏl-uissent,	nŏl-uissent,	măl-uissent.

IMPERATIVE.	INFINITIVE.
Present. nŏl-ī *or* nŏl-īto,	*Present.* vel-lĕ, nol-lĕ, mal-lĕ.
nŏl-īto,	*Perfect.* vŏl-uissĕ, nŏl-uissĕ, măl-uissĕ.
nŏl-ītōtĕ,	PRESENT PARTICIPLE.
nŏl-unto.	vŏl-ens, nŏl-ens. (wanting.)

59. Fīo, fĭĕrī, factŭs sum, *to become* or *be made,* *to happen.*

INDICATIVE.	SUBJUNCTIVE.	INDICATIVE.	SUBJUNCTIVE.
	Present.		*Future.*
S. fī-o,	fī-am,	*S.* fī-am.	
fī-s,	fī-ās.	fī-ēs.	
fī-t,	fī-ăt.	fī-ĕt.	
P. [fī-mŭs,]	fī-āmŭs.	*P.* fī-ēmŭs.	
[fī-tĭs,[	fī-ātĭs.	fī-ētĭs.	
fī-unt,	fī-ant.	fī-ent.	
	Imperfect.		*Perfect.*
S. fī-ēbam,	fī-ĕrem.	factŭs sum, etc.,	factŭs sim, etc.
fī-ēbās,	fī-ĕrēs.		*Pluperfect.*
fī-ēbăt,	fī-ĕrĕt.	factŭs ĕram, etc.,	factŭs essem, etc.
P. fī-ēbāmŭs,	fī-ĕrēmŭs.		*Future Perfect.*
fī-ēbātĭs,	fī-ĕrētĭs.	factŭs ĕro, etc.	(wanting.)
fī-ēbant,	fī-ĕrent.		

IMPERATIVE.	INFINITIVE.
Present. fī, fī-tĕ.	*Present.* fī-ĕrī.
PARTICIPLES.	*Perfect.* factum essĕ.
Perfect. factŭs (a, um).	*Future.* factum īrī.
Gerundive. făciendŭs (a, um).	

Fīo is used as the Passive of făcio.

C 2

60.   Ĕo, īvī, īrĕ, ĭtum, *to go.*

INDICATIVE.	SUBJUNCTIVE.	INDICATIVE.	SUBJUNCTIVE.
Present.		*Perfect.*	
S. ĕ-o,	e-am.	*S.* ī-vī *or* ĭ-ī,	ī-vĕrim *or* ĭ-ĕrim.
ī-s,	e-ās.	ī-vistī, etc.,	ī-vĕrĭs, etc.
ĭ-t,	e-ăt.	ī-vĭt, etc.,	ī-vĕrĭt, etc.
P. ī-mŭs,	e-āmŭs.	*P.* ī-vĭmŭs, etc.,	ī-vĕrimŭs, etc.
ī-tis,	e-ātĭs.	ī-vistĭs, etc.,	ī-vĕritĭs, etc.
e-unt,	e-ant.	ī-vērunt, etc.,	ī-vĕrint, etc.
		or ī-vērĕ.	
Imperfect.		*Pluperfect.*	
S. ī-bam,	ī-rem.	*S.* ī-vĕram *or*	ī-vissem, ī-issem,
ī-bās,	ī-rēs.	ĭ-ĕram,	*or* i-ssem.
ī-băt,	ī-rĕt.	ī-vĕr-ās, etc.,	ī-vissēs, etc.
P. ī-bāmŭs,	ī-rēmŭs.	ī-vĕrăt, etc.,	ī-vissĕt, etc.
ī-bātĭs,	ī-rētis.	*P.* ī-vĕrāmŭs, etc.,	ī-vissēmŭs, etc.
ī-bant,	ī-rent.	ī-vĕrātĭs, etc.,	ī-vissētĭs, etc.
		ī-vĕrant, etc.,	ī-vissent, etc.
Future.		*Future Perfect.*	
S. ī-bo.		*S.* ī-vĕro *or* ĭ-ĕro.	(wanting.)
ī-bĭs.		ī-vĕrĭs, etc.	
ī-bĭt.		ī-vĕrĭt, etc.	
P. ī-bĭmŭs.		*P.* ī-vĕrimŭs, etc.	
ī-bĭtĭs.		ī-vĕritĭs, etc.	
ī-bunt.		ī-vĕrint, etc.	

IMPERATIVE.	INFINITIVE.
Present. ī,	*Present.* ī-rĕ.
ī-to,	*Perfect.* ī-vissĕ, ĭissĕ, *or* issĕ.
ī-to,	*Future.* ĭ-tūrum essĕ.
i-tĕ,	
ī-tōtĕ,	PARTICIPLES.
ĕ-unto.	*Present.* ĭ-ens (*Gen.* ĕ-untĭs).
	Future. ĭ-tūrŭs (ă, um).

PRETERITIVE VERBS.

61. Preteritive Verbs are those which are used only in the Perfect tenses, and those formed from the Perfect. They are:

Coepī, *I have begun.*   Memĭnī, *I remember.*   Odī, *I hate.*

INDICATIVE.

Perfect.	coepī.	mĕmĭnī.	ōdī.
Pluperfect.	coepĕram.	mĕmĭnĕram.	ōdĕram.
Future Perfect.	coepĕrō.	mĕmĭnĕrō.	ōdĕrō.

		SUBJUNCTIVE.	
Perfect.	coepĕrĭm.	mĕmĭnĕrĭm.	ōdĕrĭm.
Pluperfect.	coepissĕm.	mĕminissĕm.	ōdissem.

IMPERATIVE.

S. mĕmentŏ.
P. mŏmentōte.

INFINITIVE.

Perfect.	coepissĕ.	memĭnisse.	ōdisse.
Future.	coeptūrŭs essĕ.		ōsūrŭs essĕ.

PARTICIPLE.

Perfect.	coeptŭs.		ōsŭs.
Future.	coeptūrŭs.		ōsūrŭs.

IMPERSONAL VERBS.

62. Impersonal Verbs are those which are used only in the Third Person Singular, and do not admit of a *personal* subject.

Their English is generally preceded by the Pronoun *it*, especially in the Active Voice; as, delectat, *it delights;* decet, *it becomes;* contingit, *it happens;* evĕnit, *it happens;* scribĭtur, *it is written*, etc.

They are thus conjugated:

INDICATIVE.

	First Conj.	Second Conj.	Third Conj.	Fourth Conj.
Present.	delectăt,	decĕt,	contingĭt,	evĕnit.
Imperfect.	delectābat,	decēbat,	contingēbat,	eveniēbat.
Future.	delectābit,	decēbit,	contĭngĕt,	evenĭet.
Perfect.	delectāvit,	decŭit,	contĭgit,	evĕnit.
Pluperfect.	delectāvĕrat,	decŭĕrat,	contĭgĕrat,	evenĕrat.
Future Perfect.	delectāvĕrit,	decŭĕrit,	contĭgĕrit,	evenĕrit.

SUBJUNCTIVE.

Present.	delectĕt,	deceăt,	contingăt,	evenĭat.
Imperfect.	delectāret,	decēret,	contingĕret,	evenīret.
Perfect.	delectāvĕrit,	decŭĕrit,	contigĕrit,	evenĕrit.
Pluperfect.	delectāvisset,	decŭisset,	contĭgisset,	evenisset.

INFINITIVE.

Present.	delectāre,	decēre,	contingĕre,	evenīre.
Perfect.	delectāvisse,	decŭisse,	contigisse,	evenisse.

REDUNDANT VERBS.

63. Redundant Verbs are such as have more than one form with one meaning.

FREQUENTATIVE VERBS.

64. Frequentative Verbs are such as express a repetition of the action denoted by their primitives. They are of the First Conjugation only, and are formed commonly from the primitive Verb by changing *um* of the supine into *o*, and sometimes the letter *a*, preceding, into *i ;* as,

habeo, *to have.*   habitum, habito, *to have often.*
pello, *to strike.*   pulsum, pulso, *to rap.*
clamo, *to cry out.*   clamatum, clamito, *to exclaim.*

INCEPTIVE VERBS.

65. Inceptive Verbs denote the commencement of the action expressed by their Primitive Verbs. They are of the Third Conjugation only, and are formed commonly from the Primitive Verb by adding *co* to the Second Person Singular of the Present Indicative Active; as,

gelo,   gelas,   gelasco, *to begin to freeze.*
rubeo,   rubes,   rubesco, *to grow red.*
tremo,   tremis,   tremisco, *to begin to tremble.*
obdormio, obdormis, obdormisco, *to fall asleep.*

DESIDERATIVE VERBS.

66. Desideratives denote a *desire* to perform the action. They are of the Fourth Conjugation, and are formed from the Supine by changing *um* into *ŭrio ;* as,

ĕs-ŭrio, *to desire to eat,*   from ĕdo, ēsum.
empt-ŭrio, *to desire to buy,*   "   ĕmo, emptum.

DIMINUTIVE VERBS.

67. Diminutives denote a *feeble* action. They are of the First Conjugation, and are formed from the Present by changing the ending into *illo ;* as,

cant-illo, *to sing feebly*, from canto.
conscrīb-illo, *to scribble*,   "   conscrībo.

ADVERBS.

68. Adverbs are words used to qualify Verbs, Adjectives, and other Adverbs. They are compared like the Adjectives from which they are formed. The termination of the Comparative is *ius*. The Superlative is formed from the Superlative of the Adjective by changing *us* into *e ;* as,

durè,	duriùs,	durissìmè ;
facìlè,	faciliùs,	facillìmè ;
acrìter,	acriùs,	acerrìmè ;
rarò,	rariùs,	rarissìmè ;
matûrè,	maturiùs,	{ maturissìmè, *or* maturrìmè.

PREPOSITIONS.

69. Prepositions express the relation between a Noun and a word before it.

CONJUNCTIONS.

70. Conjunctions are used to connect words or parts of a sentence.

INTERJECTIONS.

71. Interjections are words used to express exclamations and mental emotions.

PART III.—SYNTAX.

72. SYNTAX teaches the way in which words are arranged in sentences, and in which sentences are combined together.

73. Sentences are either Simple or Compound.

A Simple Sentence is one which contains only one Subject and one Predicate.

A Compound Sentence is a combination of two or more Simple Sentences.

74. Every Sentence contains a Subject and a Predicate.

The Subject is that of which something is affirmed.

The Predicate is that which is affirmed of the Subject; as, Terră est rŏtundă, *The earth is round.*

In this sentence "terră" is the Subject, and "est rŏtundă" is the Predicate.

75. The Subject of a Sentence is always either a Noun in the Nominative Case, or some word or words representing a Noun in the Nominative Case.

76. The Predicate is either a Verb alone, or a Verb in connection with other words which are dependent upon it.

The relations of the words in a Sentence to each other are regulated by the following Rules:

RULE I.

77. A Noun modifying the meaning of another Noun, and denoting the same thing, is put in the same Case; as, Romŭlŭs rex, *Romulus the king.*

In the example given, "rex" modifies the meaning of "Romŭlŭs," denoting the same person, and is therefore put *by apposition* in the same Case.

When the modifying Noun denotes a *different* person or thing, it is put in a different Case; as,

Sěnātus offĭcium, *The duty of the Senate.*

Urbis fundāmenta, *The foundations of the city.*

78. Adjectives, Adjective - Pronouns, and Participles agree with their Nouns in Number, Gender, and Case; as,

Vĭr saplens, *A wise man.*

Mĭ pătĕr, *O my father.*

(*a*) If the Adjective refers to two or more Nouns, it is put in the Plural Number, and in Gender prefers the Masculine before the Feminine, and the Feminine before the Neuter.

(*b*) A Collective Noun in the singular commonly has its Adjective in the plural.

79. The Relative Pronoun agrees with its antecedent in Gender, Number, and Person; the Case is determined by the construction of the clause to which it belongs; as,

Pŭer quĭ legit, *The boy who reads.*

Littĕræ quas dĕdĭ, *The letter which I gave.*

In the last example, the Relative "quas" agrees with its antecedent "littĕræ" in Gender and Number, but its Case is determined by "dedi," which is construed with the Accusative.

SYNTAX OF THE CASES.

80. The Six Cases of a Latin Noun may be distinguished as follows, viz. :

I. Nominative, denotes the Subject spoken *of.*

II. Vocative, denotes the Subject spoken *to.*

III. Accusative, denotes the Direct Object.

IV. Dative, denotes the Indirect Object.

V. Genitive, denotes the Qualification of an Adjective.

VI. Ablative, denotes the Qualification of an Adverb.

81. A Verb agrees with its subject nominative in number and Person; as,

Ego dīco, *I speak.*

(*a*) Two or more nominatives singular take the Verb in the plural, the First Person being preferred to the Second, and the Second to the Third.

(*b*) Sometimes a Verb, with two or more nominatives of different numbers and persons, agrees with one of them, and is understood with the rest.

(*c*) A Collective Noun in the singular may take a Verb in the plural.

RULE V.

82. Any Verb may have the same Case after it as before it *when both words refer to the same thing ;* as,

Ego sum discĭpŭlŭs, *I am a scholar.*

Nōvĭmŭs tē essĕ fortĕm, *We know that thou art brave.*

THE GENITIVE.

83. The Genitive performs the same functions for a word limited by it which an Adjective performs for a Noun which it qualifies.

It is commonly distinguished by the Preposition *of,* and therefore corresponds to the English Possessive Case.

Sometimes, however, it is called the Objective Genitive, and is translated by the Prepositions *to, for, from, in,* etc.

The Genitive limits the meaning of (*a*) Nouns, (*b*) Adjectives, (*c*) Verbs, (*d*) Adverbs.

RULE VI.

84. A Noun limiting the meaning of another Noun, and denoting a *different* person or thing, is put in the Genitive; as,

Fānŭm Neptūnī, *The temple of Neptune.*

In the example given, "Neptūnī" limits the meaning of "fānŭm," and confines its application to this word. It is the "*temple,*" not of man nor of any other creature, but specifically of Neptune.

This is an example of

(*a*) The Subjective Genitive, which designates a Possessor.

(*b*) The Objective Genitive designates the Object; as,

Āmŏr glōrĭæ, *Love of glory.*

Here the Genitive " glōrĭæ" designates the Object of the love, "āmŏr."

(*c*) When the limiting Genitive denotes a property, character, or quality, it has an Adjective agreeing with it, and is put either in the Genitive or in the Ablative; as,

Vĭr summæ prūdentĭæ, or,

Vĭr summâ prudentĭâ, *A man of the greatest wisdom.*

RULE VII.

85. A Noun, limiting the meaning of an Adjective for the purpose of farther specifying its meaning, is put in the Genitive; as,

Avĭdŭs laudĭs, *Desirous of praise.*

RULE VIII.

86. Nouns, Adjectives, Adjective-Pronouns, and Adverbs denoting a part, are followed by a Genitive denoting the whole; as,

Pars ĕquōrum, *A part of the horses.*

The words thus limited are usually Partitives and words used Partitively, Comparatives, Superlatives, Interrogatives, and some Numerals.

RULE IX.

87. The price of a thing stated *indefinitely* is expressed by the Genitive; as,

Magnī æstĭmābat pecūnĭam, *He esteemed money highly.*

RULE X.

88. Mĭsĕrĕor, mĭsĕresco, and sătăgo are followed by the Genitive; as,

Mĭsĕrērŏ cīvĭŭm tŭōrum, *Pity your countrymen.*

RULE XI.

89. Rĕcordŏr, Mĕmĭnī, Rĕmĭniscŏr, and Oblĭviscŏr are followed by the Genitive; as,
Mĕmĭnī vīvōrŭm, *I am mindful of the living.*

RULE XII.

90. Verbs of Accusing, Acquitting, Admonishing, Convicting, and Condemning, are followed by the Genitive;
as, Argŭĭt mŏ furtī, *He accuses me of theft.*

RULE XIII.

91. Rĕfert and Intĕrest are followed by the Genitive;
as, Rĕfert pătrĭs, *It concerns my father.*

RULE XIV.

92. The Adverbs " prĭdĭē" and " postrĭdĭē" are followed by the Genitive; as,
Postrĭdĭē ejus diēi, *The day after that day.*

THE DATIVE.

93. The Dative Case marks the Indirect Object, and is used to denote *the end towards* which any thing tends, or *the thing for* which any thing is done.

RULE XV.

94. Nouns, Adjectives, Adverbs, and Verbs are followed by the Dative denoting the object or end to or for which a thing is, or is done; as,
Tempŏrī cēdĭt, *He yields to time.*

RULE XVI.

95. Adjectives of likeness and unlikeness, friendliness, fitness, equality, and nearness, are followed by the Dative; as,
Amīcŭs tȳrannĭdī, *Friendly to tyranny.*
Simĭlis lŭpo, *Similar to a wolf.*

RULE XVII.

96. Verbs signifying to favor, please, trust, and their contraries, also to assist, command, obey, serve, resist, threaten, and be angry, are followed by the Dative; as, Illă tibī făvĕt, *She favors you.*

RULE XVIII.

97. Many Verbs compounded with these eleven Prepositions, *ad, ante, con, in, inter, ob, post, præ, pro, sub,* and *super,* are followed by the Dative; as, Annuĕ cœptīs, *Favor our undertakings.*

RULE XIX.

98. Verbs compounded with *satis, benè,* and *malè,* are followed by the Dative; as, Ět nāturæ et legibŭs satisfecit, *He satisfied both nature and the laws.*

RULE XX.

99. The Verb "est" is followed by a Dative denoting a Possessor, the thing possessed being its Subject; as, Sunt nōbīs mītĭă pōmă, *We have mellow apples.*

RULE XXI.

100. The Participle ending in *dus* is followed by the Dative of the Agent; as, Undă omnĭbŭs ēnavĭgandă, *The wave must be passed by all.*

RULE XXII.

101. Certain Adverbs and Interjections are followed by the Dative; as,
Congruĭter nātūræ, *Agreeably to nature.*
Heï mĭhĭ! *Ah me!*
Sĭbĭ constanter, *Consistently with himself.*
Væ tĭbi! *Woe to you!*

THE ACCUSATIVE.

102. The Latin Accusative is the English Objective. It is the Case of the Direct Object. It designates the person or thing actually reached and affected by the action of the Verb.

RULE XXIII.

103. The Direct Object of an Active Verb is put in the Accusative Case; as,

Lēgātōs mittūnt, *They send embassadors.*

RULE XXIV.

104. An Intransitive Verb may be followed by an Accusative of kindred signification to its own; as,

Vītăm vivěre, *To live a life.*

RULE XXV.

105. The particular part or circumstance referred to after a general affirmation is put in the Accusative for the sake of specifying or more fully explaining the word which it follows; as,

Capĭta velāmur, *We have our heads veiled.*

This is called the Synecdochical Accusative. It is of frequent occurrence in the Latin Poets, and is there denominated the Greek Accusative; as, Nudus membra, literally *Bare as to his limbs,* or *With bare limbs.*

RULE XXVI.

106. After Verbs expressing or implying motion, the name of a town or other place in which the motion terminates is put in the Accusative; as,

Vēnĭt Rōmăm, *He came to Rome.*

RULE XXVII.

107. Nouns denoting duration of time or extent of space are put in the Accusative; as,

Trēs hōrās mansĭt, *He remained three hours.*

RULE XXVIII.

108. Any Transitive Verb, together with the Accusative, may take a Genitive, or a Dative, or another Accusative, for the purpose of further explaining its meaning; as,

(*a*) Verbs of *accusing* and the like take the Accusative of the person and the *Genitive* of the crime.

(*b*) Verbs of comparing, giving, declaring, and taking away, take the Accusative of the Direct with the Dative of the Indirect Object.

(*c*) Verbs signifying to ask, teach, conceal, and some others, take two Accusatives, the first of a person and the last of a thing.

RULE XXIX.

109. When a Verb in the Active Voice is followed by two cases, the Passive Voice takes after it the latter of the two; as,

Accūsātus est prōditiōnis, *He was accused of treason.*

RULE XXX.

110. Twenty-six Prepositions are followed by the Accusative. These are, *ad, adversùs* or *adversùm, ante, apud, circa* or *circum, circĭter, cis* or *citra, contra, erga, extra, infra, inter, intra, juxta, ob, penes, per, ponè, post, præter, prope, propter, secundùm, supra, trans, ultra;* as,

Ad templŭm, *To the temple.*
Adversŭs hostēs, *Against the enemy.*

(*a*) In and Sub, expressing *motion*, are followed by the Accusative—expressing *situation*, by the Ablative; as,

In Itālĭā, *In Italy.*
In Asĭăm, *Into Asia.*

RULE XXXI.

111. The Accusative, both with and without an Interjection, is used to express an exclamation; as,

Ō condĭtĭonem misĕram! *O wretched condition!*

THE VOCATIVE.
RULE XXXII.

112. The Subject addressed is put in the Vocative; as, Quŏŭsque Catĭlīna! *How long, O Catiline!*

THE ABLATIVE.

113. The Ablative performs the same functions for the word modified by it which an Adverb performs for the word which it qualifies.

The only difference, then, between the Genitive and the Ablative is the difference between an Adjective and an Adverb.

The Ablative is commonly distinguished by the Prepositions *with, from, in,* or *by.*

RULE XXXIII.

114. The cause, manner, and instrument are expressed by the Ablative; as,

Dŭŏbus mŏdĭs fĭt, *It is done in two ways.*

RULE XXXIV.

115. The price of a thing, stated *definitely,* is expressed by the Ablative; as,

Vīlĕ est vīgintī mĭnīs, *It is cheap at twenty minœ.*

RULE XXXV.

116. The Comparative Degree, without a Conjunction, is followed by the Ablative; as,

Pĕrennĭŭs ærĕ, *More durable than brass.*

RULE XXXVI.

117. Opus and ŭsus are followed by the Ablative; as, Auctorĭtātĕ tŭā nōbĭs opŭs est, *We need your authority.*

Usus est tua mĭhĭ opĕra, *I need your aid.*

Est opus pecūniā, *There is need of money.*

RULE XXXVII.

118. Dignus, indignus, contentus, præditus, captus, and fretus, are followed by the Ablative; as,
Dignŭs laudĕ, Worthy of praise.

RULE XXXVIII.

119. Utor, abutor, fruor, fungor, potior, and vescor, are followed by the Ablative; as,
Hīs vocĭbus ūsă est, She used these words.

RULE XXXIX.

120. Perfect Participles denoting origin are often followed by the Ablative of the source; as,
Mæcēnās ătăvīs ēdĭtŏ rēgĭbus, Mœcenas descended from ancestral kings.

RULE XL.

121. Adjectives of Plenty and Want, and Verbs signifying to abound and to be destitute, are followed by the Ablative; as,
Dŏmus plēnă servīs, A house full of servants.
Urbs rĕdundăt mīlĭtĭbŭs, The city is full of soldiers.

RULE XLI.

122. The time at which an event occurs is expressed by the Ablative; as,
Hōc tēmpŏrĕ, At this time.

RULE XLII.

123. A Noun and a Participle, whose Case depends upon no other word in a sentence, is said to be in the Ablative Absolute; as,
Lūpŭs, stīmŭlantĕ fămĕ, captăt ŏvīlĕ, The wolf, hunger inciting, seeks the fold.
Tēlīs conjectīs, By pouring in darts.
Natūra ducĕ, Nature being our guide.

RULE XLIII.

124. The Place *in* which any thing occurs, and the Place *from* which any thing proceeds, are expressed in the Ablative; as,

Fŭĭt Athēnīs, *He was in Athens.*

Fūgĭt Cŏrinthō, *He fled from Corinth.*

Certain names of Places, of the 1st and 2d Declensions, *at* which any thing occurs, are expressed, *apparently*, in the Genitive Case; as,

Quĭd Rōmæ făcĭăm, *What can I do at Rome?*

These are really *not Genitives at all*, but only old Ablatives. In the earlier stages of the language, the Genitive and the Ablative terminated alike. When, in other words, the Ablative underwent a change, in these words it retained its old Genitive form.

The same principle applies to the Genitives dŏmī, mīlī-tĭæ, bellī, and hūmī; as,

Dŏmī mīlĭtĭæquĕ, *At home and in the field.*

RULE XLIV.

125. Ten Prepositions are followed by the Ablative: these are, *a, ab,* or *abs, absque, coram, cum, de, e* or *ex, præ, pro, sine, tenus.*

SYNTAX OF THE VERB.

THE INDICATIVE MOOD.

126. The Indicative is used to affirm or to deny in both dependent and independent Sentences. It is the Mood employed to represent realities or facts; as,

Āmo, *I love.*

Docĕo, *I teach.*

THE SUBJUNCTIVE MOOD.

127. The Subjunctive Mood never represents facts, but only conceptions of the mind.

It is employed to denote,

D

(1st.) The Purpose, Object, or Result of a preceding Proposition, in connection with *ut, ne, quo, quin,* and *quominus ;* as,

Ēnītītūr ŭt vincăt, *He strives that he may conquer.*

(2d.) Something which is not real, but *desirable,* in connection with *utinam, ut, si,* and *O si ;* as,

Ūtīnam possĕm,*Would that I were able.*

(3d.) A *condition* upon which something depends, in connection with *dum, modo, si, nisi, velut,* and others; as,

Sī volŭissĕt dīmĭcassĕt, *If he had wished, he would have fought.*

(4th.) A concession of a proposition in connection with *licet, quamvis,* and *etsi ;* as,

Etsī nĭhĭl hăbĕăt ĭn se glōrĭă, tămĕn virtūtĕm sĕquĭtūr, *Though glory may have nothing in itself, yet it follows virtue.*

(5th.) A cause on account of which, or a time at which, something is or is done, in connection with *quod, quia, quoniam, dum, donec,* and *quoad ;* as,

Socrātēs accūsātŭs est, quŏd corrumpĕrĕt jŭvĕntūtĕm, *Socrates was accused because he corrupted the youth.*

(6th.) Dependent clauses and indirect questions are usually expressed in the Subjunctive Mood when they report the thoughts of the speaker in words not his own; as,

Quĭs ĕgo sĭm mē rogĭtās? *Do you ask me who I am?*

IMPERATIVE MOOD.

128. The Imperative Mood is used to give utterance to a command, a prohibition, an exhortation, or an entreaty; as,   Nōscĕ tē, *Know thyself.*

THE INFINITIVE MOOD.

129. The Infinitive is used merely to state the meaning of the Verb, without limitation of person or number. It is regulated by the following Rules, viz.:

RULE XLV.

130. The Subject of the Infinitive Mood is put in the Accusative; as,

Gaudĕo tĕ valērĕ, *I am glad that you are well.*

RULE XLVI.

131. The Infinitive may be used as a Verbal Noun, and hence become the *subject* or the *object* of another Verb; as,

Grātŭm est tēcŭm ambŭlārĕ, *It is pleasant to walk with you.*

Părăt bellŭm gĕrĕrĕ, *He prepares to wage war.*

PARTICIPLES.

132. A Participle is a part of the Verb which expresses its meaning considered as a quality. It differs from an Adjective in conveying the additional idea of time.

RULE XLVII.

133. Participles govern the Case of their own Verbs; as,

Āmāns vīrtūtĕm, *Loving virtue.*

GERUNDS.

134. The Gerund is a Verbal Noun having Four Cases, the Genitive, Dative, Accusative, and Ablative, which are construed like the Cases of other Nouns.

RULE XLVIII.

135. Gerunds, like Verbs, have both Direct and Indirect Objects.

136. Sometimes the Direct Object is put in the Case of the Gerund, which in this instance is changed into the Future Passive Participle, and made to agree with the Object. The Gerund is then called a Gerundive; as,

Studium { agrum colendī (a), *Gerund,* } *The pursuit of*
         { agrī colendī (b), *Gerundive,* } *tilling the soil.*

SUPINES.

137. The Supine is a Verbal Noun having two Cases, the Accusative ending in *um*, the Ablative in *u*.

ADVERBS.
RULE XLIX.

138. Adverbs qualify the meaning of Verbs, Adjectives, and other Adverbs.

CONJUNCTIONS.
RULE L.

139. Conjunctions commonly connect similar Moods and Cases.

PART IV.—PROSODY.

140. PROSODY is the science of Versification.

141. Latin Poetry is regulated by the quantity of the syllables in the words composing it.

142. The quantity of a syllable is the time taken to pronounce it.

143. A combination of syllables, whether belonging to the same or to different words, is called a FOOT.

144. The following Feet occur most frequently; viz.,

Spondee=two long syllables (– –); as, Cōndūnt.

Trochee or Choree=one long and one short (– ⌣); as Ātqŭe.

Iambus=one short and one long (⌣ –); as, Mĕī.

Pyrrhic=two short syllables (⌣ ⌣); as, Pătĕr.

Dactyl=one long and two short (– ⌣ ⌣); as, Tĕrrŭīt.

Anapæst=two short and one long (⌣ ⌣ –); as, Dŏmĭnī.

Tribrach=three short syllables (⌣ ⌣ ⌣); as, Ălĭtĕr.

Bacchius=one short and two long (⌣ – –); as, Ămāndō.

Smaller Ionic=two short and two long (⌣ ⌣ – –); as, Prŏpĕrābānt.

Choriambus=one long, two short, and one long (– ⌣ ⌣ –); as, Ōppŏsĭtīs.

A single syllable occurring in the middle or at the end of a line is called a long Catalectic syllable.

145. METRE is the arrangement of these Feet in accordance with regular Rules.

146. A VERSE is a single line of Poetry.

147. SCANNING is the division of a verse into Feet.

148. SYNALŒPHA is the cutting off of a vowel in the *end* of a word before another vowel in the *beginning* of the word which follows it; as, Sive inopes is scanned Siv' inopes.

149. ECTHLIPSIS is cutting off of final m with the preceding vowel when the next word begins with a vowel; as, Præsĭdĭ*um* ĕt is scanned Præsĭdĭ' ĕt.

150. Synæresis is the contraction of two syllables into one; as, Phaëthon is by Synæresis Phæthon.

151. Diæresis is the separation of one syllable into two; as, Phæthon is by Diæresis Phaëthon. Two dots above the latter letter mark the occurrence of the figure.

A knowledge of these terms, together with a thorough acquaintance with the following rules of quantity, is necessary before the pupil is prepared to scan Latin verse.

RULES OF QUANTITY.

RULE I.

152. A vowel before another vowel or a Diphthong is short by Position.

RULE II.

Contracted Syllables and Diphthongs are Long.

RULE III.

A vowel before any two consonants, or before the letters j, x, or z, is long by Position.

RULE IV.

Derivative words retain the quantity of the words from which they are derived.

RULE V.

Compound words retain the quantity of the words which compose them.

INCREMENTS.

1. A Noun is said to *increase* when in any of its cases it has more syllables than in the Nominative Singular.

2. A Verb is said to *increase* when it has in any part more syllables than in the Second Person Singular of the Present Indicative Active.

3. If a word has but one increment, it is the penult; if two, the antepenult is called the first increment and the

penult the second; if three, the syllable before the antepenult is called the first, the antepenult the second, and the penult the third; as,

sermo, ser-mŏn-ĭs, ser-mŏn-ĭ-bŭs, ĭt-ĭn-ĕr-ĭ-bŭs.

RULE VI.

In the Increments of Nouns, a and o are long, e, i, u, and y are short; as,

Animal, Animālis.   Sermo, Sermōnis.   Opus, Opĕris.

RULE VII.

In the Increments of Verbs, a, e, and o are long, i and u are short; but

In the First Increment of all the Present and Imperfect Tenses—

(1) In the Third Conjugation, and before the syllables ram, rim, and ro, e is *short;* and

(2) In the First Increment of the Fourth Conjugation i is *long;* as,

Amo,	Amas,	Amābam.
Doceo,	Doces,	Docēbo.
Facio,	Facis,	Facitōte.

RULE VIII.

Penults in ābrum, ūbrum, ācrum, and ātrum; in ōsus, ātum, ĭtum, and ūtum; in ūdus, āris, āre, and ēlus, are long.

RULE IX.

Penults in ca, do, ga, go, ba, po, pa, ma, tus, le, les, lis, na, ne, ni, nis, dex, dix, mex, mix, lex, rex, al, and ar, are long.

RULE X.

Penults in ānus, ēnus, ōnus, and ūnus; in āna, ēna, ōna, and ūna; and in ēlus, ēla, and ēlum, are long.

RULE XI.

Penults in ārus, ōrus, ăvus, ĭvus, ates, itis, otis, ata, eta, ota, and uta, are long.

RULE XII.

Penults in ăcus, ĭcus, and ĭcum, and Nouns in ĭta, are short.

RULE XIII.

Penults in ĭdus, ĭmus, ўmus, and diminutives in ilus, olus, ulus, and words of more than two syllables in ulus, ula, ulum, are short.

RULE XIV.

Penults in ĕtas, ĭtas, ĭter, and ĭtus are short.

RULE XV.

Perfects and Supines of two Syllables make the first Syllable long, though that of the Present may be short.

RULE XVI.

A, e, o, and u before final mus, mum, men, and mentum, are long.

RULE XVII.

Before final ro, ror, rus, ra, and rum, e is short.

RULE XVIII.

Penults before v, and in inus, except in Adjectives of time or material, are long.

RULE XIX.

Monosyllables are long.

RULE XX.

Polysyllables ending in vowels make the termination

a, in undeclined words and Verbs, LONG;
a, in other declined words, short;
e and y, short;
i and u, long; and
o, common.

RULE XXI.

Final syllables in b, d, l, n, r, and t, are short.

RULE XXII.

Final c is long.

RULE XXIII.

Final as, es, and os are long; is, us, and ys, short.

RULE XXIV.

The last syllable in every line is common.

To these Rules are many exceptions, which can only be learned by practice.

Such cases as fall under no rule are said to be determined by AUTHORITY—i. e., the authority of the Poets.

HORATIAN METRES.

153. The following table contains the first words in the first stanza of each Ode. The figures annexed refer to the corresponding figures in the section following, in which the name of the metre is stated, with stanzas accompanying, showing the feet of which the line is composed, and the order in which they occur:

Æli, vetusto	No. 1	Cur me querelis	No. 1
Æquam memento	1	Delicta majorum	1
Albi, ne doleas	5	Descende cœlo	1
Altera jam teritur	13	Dianam, teneræ	6
Angustam, amici	1	Diffugere nives	14
At, O deorum	4	Dive, quem proles	2
Audivere, Lyce	6	Divis orte bonis	5
Bacchum in remotis	1	Donarem pateras	7
Beatus ille	4	Donec gratus eram	3
Cœlo supinas	1	Eheu ! fugaces	1
Cœlo tonantem	1	Est mihi nonum	2
Cùm tu, Lydi	3	Et thure et fidibus	3

1. Two greater Alcaics, one Archilochian iambic dimeter hypermeter, and one lesser Alcaic; as,

Vĭdēs | ŭt āl|tā | stēt nĭvĕ cān|dĭdūm
Sōrāc|tĕ, nēc | jām | sūstĭnĕānt | ŏnūs

Sīlvǣ | lăbō|rāntēs, | gĕlŭ|quē
Flūmĭnă | cōnstĭtĕ|rĭnt ă|cūto.—*Lib.* 1, 9.

Greater Alcaic=two Iambi (the first of which may be changed for a Spondee), a Catalectic syllable, a Choriambus, and an Iambus.

Archilochian=four Iambi, admitting of Spondees in the 1st and 3d places, followed by a Catalectic syllable.

Lesser Alcaic=two Dactyls, followed by two Trochees.

2. Three Sapphics and one Adonic; as,

> Jăm să|tĭs tēr|rĭs nĭvĭs | ātquĕ | dīrœ
> Grāndĭ|nĭs mī|sīt pătĕr, | ĕt, rŭ|bēntĕ
> Dēxtĕ|ra săc|rās jăcŭ|lātŭs | ārcĕs,
> Tērrŭĭt | ūrbēm.—*Lib.* 1, 2.

Sapphic=a Trochee, a Spondee, a Dactyl, followed by two Trochees.

Adonic=a Dactyl and a Spondee.

3. One Glyconic and one Asclepiadic; as,

> Sīc tē | Dīvă pŏtēns | Cȳpri,
> Sīc frā|trēs Hĕlĕnǣ, | lūcĭdă sĭd|ĕra.—*Lib.* 1, 3.

Glyconic=a Spondee, a Choriambus, and an Iambus.

Asclepiadic=a Spondee, two Choriambi, and an Iambus.

4. One Iambic trimeter and one Iambic dimeter; as,

> Ībĭs | Lĭbūr|nĭs ĭn|tĕr āl|tă nā|vĭum,
> Ămī|cĕ, prō|pūgnā|cŭla.—*Epod.* 1.

Iambic trimeter=six Iambi, admitting Spondees into the 1st, 3d, and 5th places.

Iambic dimeter=four Iambi, admitting Spondees into the 1st and 3d places.

5. Three Asclepiadics and one Glyconic; as,

> Scrībē|rĭs Vărĭō | fōrtĭs, ĕt hōs|tĭum
> Vīctōr, | Mǣŏnĭi | cārmĭnĭs āl|ĭti,
> Quām rēm | cūmquĕ fĕrōx | nāvĭbŭs āut | ĕquis
> Mīlēs, | tē dŭcĕ, gēss|ĕrit.—*Lib.* 1, 6.

(See No. 3.)

6. Two Asclepiadics, one Pherecratic, and one Glyconic; as,

> Dīānām, tĕnĕrœ, dīcĭtĕ vīrgĭnes:
> Īntōnsūm, pŭĕrī, dīcĭtĕ Cȳnthĭum,
> Lātō|nāmquĕ sŭprē|mo
> Dīlēctăm pĕnĭtŭs Jŏvi.—*Lib.* 1, 21.

Pherecratic = a Spondee, a Choriambus, and a Catalectic syllable.

7. The Asclepiadic alone; as,

Mæcēnās ătăvīs ēdĭtĕ rēgĭbus.—*Lib.* 1, 1.

8. One Dactylic hexameter and one Dactylic tetrameter *a posteriōre;* as,

Lāudā|būnt ălĭ|ī clā|rām Rhŏdŏn, | āut Mĭtȳ|lēnen,
Āut Ēphĕ|sūm, bĭmă|rīsvĕ Cŏ|rīnthi.—*Lib.* 1, 7.

The Datcylic hexameter, or Heroic Verse, is used in narrative and pastoral poetry. This is the metre of the Poems of Virgil, of the Satires and Epistles of Horace, of the Metamorphoses of Ovid, and of the Iliad and Odyssey of Homer in Greek. It consists of six feet, all either Dactyls or Spondees. The fifth is always a Dactyl, and the Sixth a Spondee. Each of the first four is a Dactyl or a Spondee, which is to be determined by the pupil from the quantity of the syllables composing them.

The Dactylic tetrameter *a posteriōre* consists of the last four feet of a Dactylic hexameter.

9. The Choriambic pentameter alone; as,

Tū nē | quæsĭĕrīs, | scīrĕ nĕfās, | quēm mĭhĭ, quem | tĭbi.—*Lib.* 1, 11.

Choriambic pentameter = a Spondee, three Choriambi, and an Iambus.

10. One Dactylic hexameter and one Iambic dimeter; as,

Nōx ĕrăt, | ēt cœ|lō fūl|gēbāt | lūnă sĕ|rēno
Intēr | mĭnō|ră sĭd|ĕra.—*Epod.* 15.

11. The Iambic trimeter alone.
(See No. 4.)

12. One Choriambic dimeter and one Choriambic tetrameter, with a variation; as,

Lȳdĭă, dīc, | pĕr ōmnes
Tē Dĕōs ō|rō, Sȳbărīn | cŭr prŏpĕrās|ămāndo.—*Lib.* 1, 8.

Choriambic dimeter = a Choriambus and a Bacchius.

Choriambic tetrameter = three Choriambi and a Bacchius.

13. One Dactylic hexameter and one Iambic trimeter without Spondees; as,

Āltĕrā jăm tĕrĭtŭr bĕllĭs cīvīlĭbŭs ætas.;
Sŭĭs ĕt ĭpsā Rōmā vīrĭbŭs rŭit.—*Epod.* 16.

(See above, No. 8, 4.)

14. One Dactylic hexameter and one dactylic penthemimeris; as,

Dīffūgērĕ nĭvĕs : rĕdĕŭnt jăm grămĭnā cāmpīs,
Ārbŏrĭ|būsquĕ cŏ|mæ.—*Lib.* 4, 7.

Dactylic penthemimeris=the first five half feet of a hexameter—usually=two Dactyls and a Catalectic syllable.

15. One Iambic trimeter, one Dactylic trimeter catalectic, and one Iambic dimeter; as,

Pĕttī, nĭhīl mē, sīcŭt āntĕā, jŭvat
Scrībĕrĕ | vērsĭcŭ|los,
Amōrĕ pērcŭlsūm grăvi.—*Epod.* 11.

The second line consists of the first five half feet of a Hexameter, but the first and second feet are commonly Dactyls.

(See above.)

16. One Dactylic hexameter, one Iambic dimeter, and one Dactylic penthemimeris; as,

Hōrrĭdā tēmpēstās cœlūm cōntrāxĭt ; ĕt īmbres
Nĭvēsquĕ dēdūcūnt Jōvem :
Nūnc mărĕ, nūnc sĭldæ.—*Epod.* 13.

(See above.)

17. One Archilochian heptameter and one Iambic trimeter catalectic; as,

Sōlvĭtŭr | ācrĭs hī|ēms grā|tā vĭcĕ | vērĭs | ēt Fā|vōnî,
Trăhūnt|quĕ sĭc|cās māch|ĭnæ | cărīn|as.—*Lib.* 1, 4.

The Archilochian heptameter consists of the first four feet of a hexameter, the fourth being always a Dactyl, followed by three Trochees.

The Iambic trimeter catalectic is the Iambic trimeter, lacking the last syllable.

18. One Iambic dimeter acephalous and one Iambic trimeter catalectic; as,

Nōn ĕbŭr nĕque aūrĕum
Mĕā rĕnīdĕt ĭn dŏmō lăcūnar.—*Lib.* 2, 18.

Iambic dimeter acephalous is the Iambic dimeter lacking the first syllable.

Iambic trimeter catalectic. See No. 17.

19. The Ionic *a minōre* alone ; as,

Mĭsĕrārum ēst | nĕque ămōrī | dărĕ lūdūm | nĕquĕ dūlcī.—*Lib.* 3, 12.

The Ionic *a minōre* consists generally of three or four smaller Ionic feet.

THE END.

www.ingramcontent.com/pod-product-compliance
Lightning Source LLC
Chambersburg PA
CBHW032352020726
47499CB00008B/2708